THE SPIDER:
THE SPIDER AND THE WAR EMPEROR

THE MASTER OF MEN!

SPIDER®

THE SPIDER AND
THE WAR EMPEROR

By Grant Stockbridge

POPULAR PUBLICATIONS • 2025

PUBLISHING HISTORY

"The Spider and the War Emperor" originally appeared in the May, 1940 (Vol. 20, No. 4) issue of *The Spider* magazine. Copyright 2025 by Argosy Communications, Inc. All rights reserved.

CHAPTER 1
WHEN DEATH COMMANDS

ALL BUT one on the Chinatown bus were obviously tourists. They giggled and gawked and gaped at the points of interest announced along the sightseeing route... But the man on the back seat looked at nothing.

He sat with his shoulders a little hunched, his gloved hands clasped on the head of his cane. And, until the bus stopped at Haven Street, he did not once lift his head. He climbed out then... not to follow the others trouping toward the famous Oriental joss house of the Yellow Dragon—but to walk alone up the narrow pavements of that twisting Chinatown street.

Chinese men stepped from his path and, at each one, the stranger looked piercingly with eyes that were imperious beneath smooth gray brows. He walked with his shoulders braced, with his chin thrust out angrily.

When he had covered one side of Haven Street, he crossed and came down the other. His stride now was longer, angrier, and a touch of color lay hotly on each cheekbone.

He was passing a dusty curio shop, when a hiss, like the angry blowing of a disturbed snake, stopped him. He turned swiftly toward the shop, and the aged Chinese who sat upon a stool just outside the door, let a wisp of smoke drift insolently between withered lips. His eyes were closed, and behind him, the curio shop showed a single, dim yellow lamp.

The stranger rasped out an oath, jerked his cane. "I am Carter France," he said harshly. "If you want me, say so!"

The eyes of the old Chinese opened and by that single act, his face was transformed from moldering death to evil life. The eyes were small and black and shining, and there was cruel laughter behind them.

"Mr. France would be wise to look at some of my poor curios," the Chinese said—and there was both invitation and threat in his piping voice.

Carter France snorted and strode into the shop. He slapped the door open with a gloved palm, his back stiff, head thrown up in challenge. The old Chinese doddered to his feet. He did not bother to pick up his chair, but he carried his pipe delicately between monkey-like fingers. He followed Carter France inside the shop.

After a while he came out again, alone.

IN THE next fifteen minutes, two other persons stopped at the hiss of a snake and went inside to look at curios. One was a bitter-jawed young man, with angry, fear-haunted eyes. Another was a girl. Her steps were uncertain as she went through the low door into the gloomy shop. Her eyes, enormous in a dead-white face, had the shine of terror.

And none of the three came out.

A policeman paced deliberately down the block, paused to peer at the aged Chinese, smoking on his stool.

"Is everything all right, Uncle Fu?" he asked.

The Chinese hissed contentedly between his teeth. "Everything is perfect, officer," he said.

The policeman lifted his nightstick to the visor of his cap. It might have been a casual, friendly gesture—or the salute to a master! He paced on, slowly.

The aged Chinese labored to his feet once more. He stepped inside his door and the rasp of bolts was heavy as he locked it. His step was meditative, slow. He went back through the curtains which cut off the rear of his shop. His fingers brushed the edge of a temple bell and it vibrated into slow, whirring sound.

There was another sound then, the clean, oil-smooth movement of machinery. A wall-hung rug was brushed aside, and a towering Mongol, naked to the waist, bowed his forehead to the floor.

"Hail, Master!" he whispered. "All is ready for the All-High, the All-Powerful, the Mighty!"

The aged Chinese clucked out a syllable and went through the opening. As he moved, his shoulders lost their stoop, and his stride lengthened into the pacing of a panther. When he entered the room where golden silks draped the walls, his face was no longer a wrinkled mummy-mask. It was as alive as those black, bitter eyes—and as evil!

He seated himself upon the dragon throne. His palms whispered together.

As quickly as if his hands had touched some hidden mechanism, the golden curtains at the far end of the throne room swung apart with a faint metallic rustle. Flooded by the tinted lights from within, its lone occupant stood out boldly.

It was the man who had called himself Carter France!

For an instant, he stood there motionless, then he strode toward the dragon throne. There was dignity and fury in his stride, but he assumed a challenging posture before the man on the throne.

"I came," Carter France said harshly, "not because I am afraid of you, but so that I could learn your identity to report to the police!"

The man on the throne sat motionless. Not even his eyelids blinked. His hands rested passively on the curved necks of the dragons that formed the arms.

"Yes," he said sibilantly, "it was your courage I counted on to bring you here, Carter France. I will tell you what I require of you. You control certain patents, certain secrets for the special one-process tempering of steel. It produces, I understand, a steel with the hardness of high-carbon metal, but with the elasticity of a finely tempered product. You will surrender these secrets to me. You will be allowed to continue the manufacture... for the nations I shall designate. For all others, you will produce an inferior grade of metal which will fail the tests."

He paused, and his rheumy, evil eyes shut dreamily. "So that you will continue to obey my will you, Carter France, will send your daughter to me at once—as hostage!"

CARTER FRANCE'S thinly determined lips moved in a slight smile. He looked about him deliberately.

"This mummery may impress others," he said drily. "To me, it looks like a setup out of a Grade C motion picture."

The man on the throne blinked slowly, clapped his palms together. The silken curtains rustled, and three of the powerful, half-naked Mongols strode into the room. Knives were thrust into their belts. They dropped to their knees and struck their foreheads against the floor thrice.

"Thy commands, Mighty One!" they whispered.

Carter France wheeled at the sight of the men, stepped aside so that he could confront the three of them together. His hands were together upon his stick. He twisted the cane's head slightly, and the thin, cold glitter of steel showed—a sword cane! He waited.

"Go to the street, my slaves," said the man on the throne. "Bring in the most intelligent white man you can find. Quickly!"

Carter France frowned as the men backed across the throne room, and ducked out beyond the golden curtains. He glared at the expressionless mask of the man on the throne.

"I have delivered the message I came to give," France said shortly. "I will go now! Let anyone try to stop me at his peril!" He snapped his two hands apart, and the long blade glimmered in his fist. He strode in the wake of the three Mongols, whipped aside the curtains... and was staring at a blank wall!

"The room is sealed," whispered the man on the throne, "until I choose to open it."

Carter France whipped around toward the throne. He walked toward it with long, slouching strides, the sword reaching before him. With a lithe movement that betrayed the firm muscles of his body, he presented the needle point to the throat of his captor!

"You will unseal the room," he ordered coldly.

The man on the throne did not speak, nor move, except that his black eyes widened in unblinking focus upon Carter France.

The steel man spoke again, angrily. "You heard me, you yellow fool! Order the doors unsealed, or I'll slit your throat!"

For seconds, after that, there was no further word. The eyes of the man on the throne stretched wider. They seemed enormous. His lips parted drily.

"You may call me *Master,*' Carter France," he whispered.

Carter France's jaw muscles swelled visibly under his healthily tanned skin. His sword arm was rigid, his body poised for the thrust. Perspiration popped out on his upper lip and beneath his eyes. His lips parted slowly, showing the gleam of locked teeth. A word issued from his dry throat, through his locked teeth, as if another person were within his body, speaking through his vocal mechanism.

And the word was, *"Master!"*

NOT UNTIL then did the man on the throne, the Master, speak again. He said, "Put your sword away, Carter France. It would bend against my flesh, but it would not pierce."

A strong shudder shook Carter France. His sword arm fell stiffly as a stick. Under the thrust of the Master's eyes, he retreated three heavy, laborious steps. His movements were mechanical, like those of a sleepwalker.

The Master's lips moved faintly. The twist might have been an ugly smile. "I could compel your obedience in this way, Carter

France," he said softly, "but it would be an unintelligent obedience. I prefer to have you worship… of your own free will!"

Carter France struggled to speak, and no words came from between his pallid lips. The sword hung useless in his hand. A minute dragged past. He heard again the rustle of silken curtains, and the three Mongols thrust forward a man—a young defiant man who cursed angrily at the Master on his throne.

"Look at this man, Carter France," said the Master, softly. "Study the well-formed jaw, the thin intelligence of the nose, the well-placed, angry eyes. I shall demonstrate my powers upon him, Carter France. I shall show you the thing you must face— if you any longer resist my orders. Wake up, France! Wake up, and pay heed!"

Carter France started, looked down at the sword in his hand, and at the man on the throne. A tremor ran over his body, and the line of his jaw was suddenly lax and old.

"Yes… Master," he whispered.

At the Master's order, the struggling man was brought close to the throne. Carter France felt his own trembling increase. Unreasoning horror dried his throat. He remembered achingly that moment when he had tensed every muscle in his body in an effort to send his sword through the throat of the… the Master—and had failed! He did not want to look at the throne, but fascination drew his eyes. He saw that the Master's unblinking black eyes were fixed upon those of the prisoner… and the man was no longer struggling.

The Master removed his eyes from the man to glance toward Carter France. "He was not so intelligent as I supposed," he said deliberately. "A very easy... victim. It would require only a little longer to dispose of you, Carter France, as this young man shall presently be disposed of. Out of the East I come with powers beyond the knowledge of this emasculated West... This man on whom I have loosed a portion of my will... *soon will become an imbecile!*"

Carter France's eyes widened with shock. He did not believe the thing he heard. He could not believe either that, a few moments before, he had stood with his sword against the throat of this monster—and could not drive it home!

But his eyes held rigidly to the body of the captive before the Master's throne and, even as he watched, a change was coming over the youngster. There was a new laxness in his limbs. The stiffness was gone from his shoulders and his whole body was flaccid.

Carter France spoke hoarsely. "No!" he said, "No, I tell you!"

The man, released of the restraining hands of the Mongols, went lax at the knees. His hands dangled. He turned limply around and lifted his head to stare at the tinted lights. His jaw was loose, and moisture was about his lips. His eyes were as shallow and senseless as a cat's.

"No!" Carter France gasped.

The man's head swung toward him. An imbecilic grin moved his lips. He made a sound in his throat. It was not a word, but a meaningless noise such as an infant might make. He shambled toward Carter France... and France cursed horribly. He whirled about and ran. He tore at the silk curtains... and there were only solid walls behind them. He beat at the wall with his fists. Behind him, again, he heard the *sound.*

With a cry, Carter France whipped around. The imbecilic face of the man was grinning up into his!

"Get away from me!" France shouted. He put the point of his sword against the man's chest.

Once more, the man made a sound in his throat. This time it made a fragment of sense. He said, "Pretty… Pretty!"

He closed his hand tightly around the blade of the sword. It cut him and blood squeezed out between his fingers. He stared at Carter France in bewilderment. His face puckered up like a child's. Tears slid down his cheeks. He began to sob.

France shouted, "For God's sake, take him away! *Take him away!*"

THE MASTER laughed on his throne, and the sound was like tearing silk. "No need to take him away, Carter France," said the Master. "He will soon be dead! Look, Carter France! *Look at the thing you will become—unless you obey!*"

Carter France screamed, *"No!"* He beat the wall with his futile hands. He tore at the silken curtains, and his nails worked through the fingers of his gloves. They bled.

"Look, Carter France!" whispered the Master.

France fought against the order. He fought his own body,

which was turning about. He fought his eyes, which insisted on staring at this man who had been so boldly angry a few minutes before… at the imbecile!

The youth's legs would no longer support him. He sagged to his knees, and his face held the emptiness of a newborn baby's. His hands and legs had the same lack of direction. He rolled on his back on the floor, waving his knotted fists, making hoarse, meaningless sounds.

Carter France broke free of the horrid fascination that held him. He ran toward the throne, shouting, waving his thin-bladed sword.

"Damn you!" he cried. "Damn you, you're a monster! You can't do this sort of thing here! Not in America! I'll destroy you! I'll…" He stopped short, well out of reach of the throne. Anger still made his eyes fiery, but he went no nearer. "I'll report this atrocity to the police!" he said.

The Master blinked at him. "On that score, too," he said softly, "I have prepared a little demonstration. The policeman has been called in from the beat, and…" He rasped his palms together and the silk drapes whipped aside on the far side of the room. It

13

was like the lifting of curtains on a stage. There was a girl there, cowering against a stone wall. She was white with terror.

"Miriam!" Carter France gasped. "My secretary! Damn it, let her go! I tell you to let her go!"

As he shouted, a policeman stepped into the lighted area, revolver in hand. France started toward him, shouting.

"Officer!" he cried. "Arrest this man! He has just driven a man crazy! He has threatened me, taken my secretary prisoner!"

His voice echoed against the silk-draped walls and lost its power there. It seemed to close in about his own ears. He was shouting… but the Master whispered, and his whisper was louder than all the outcry of Carter France. He spoke to the policeman.

"Kill the girl," he said calmly.

The policeman wheeled, whipped up his revolver. Miriam's scream choked off in her throat. It was blown back into her lungs by the blast of the revolver. She was bent double by the punch of the lead. Her arms pulled in, her head bent forward. She slid to the floor that way, rolled over and was motionless… dead.

The Master's words whispered inside Carter France's brain. "I am invincible," he said. "The police do my bidding, even to the point of murder. With my will, I can drive a man to madness, can turn him into a puling infant, can rob him of his life! Remember what you have seen here, Carter France… And send your daughter, and your submission to me by this time tomorrow night. You have seen the penalties of disobedience… Take him away."

CARTER FRANCE wasn't quite sure how he had arrived there, but when next he was conscious of his whereabouts, he found himself standing stiffly before the bar at the Marlton Club. There was a bottle of brandy, half-emptied, on the bar before him. He started when a voice spoke at his elbow.

"You looked worried, old man," it said. "Anything I can do to help you?"

Carter France's head whipped stiffly around. His pent breath gusted forth. "Oh, it's you, Wentworth," he said heavily. "No… No, I'm not worried. Thanks."

He turned back to the bar, and his eyes probed into the mirror behind it. His face was a dingy gray, and horror seemed to have widened his eyes permanently. He could not get the staring glisten of fear out of them. And his hand trembled as he poured another brandy.

"No, I'm not worried," he said again, tonelessly.

He was tautly conscious of the man beside him, of the sympathy in the keen gray-blue eyes of Richard Wentworth. Wentworth was a good friend of the Police Commissioner, Stanley Kirkpatrick. For that matter Kirkpatrick was a member of the club. Perhaps….

Carter France's head turned stiffly. His staring eyes met the kindly gaze of Richard Wentworth.

"Is Kirkpatrick in the club?" France asked hoarsely.

Wentworth shook his head. His face showed only his warm interest, but behind that casual mask, his brain was probing the meaning of France's strange behavior. France was a temperate man. A glass or two of wine was his usual limit. Tonight, he had stood at the bar and drunk six straight brandies, one after the other, with the regularity of clock-work. The alcohol had put a

15

spotty pink in his gray cheeks, but it seemed to leave no other apparent effect.

"I'm sure Kirkpatrick will be glad to come here, at once," Wentworth said quietly, "if you want to see him."

France appeared not to see Wentworth. His eyes were fixed somewhere beyond, but the real picture he saw was in his brain.

"No, no," he said hopelessly. "It wouldn't work. It would do no good."

Wentworth leaned his elbows casually on the bar, offered his slim platinum cigarette case.

"Smoke, France? I can recommend them. A special blend of Turkish and Virginia…. Perhaps you would care to give me the gist of your troubles. I have a rather close contact with Kirkpatrick, you know."

France's eyes were a little more normal. He reached out a suddenly shaking hand for a cigarette. "The police could do nothing," he muttered. "That's fairly proved… God, Wentworth! I can't believe… what I know is true. I'm afraid, I…" He broke off, and his eyes were staring wildly into the mirror. Wentworth followed his gaze, straightening swiftly. But he saw nothing to frighten a man like France. It was only that a uniformed policeman had come to a halt on the pavement outside, chatting with the club's doorman. It was true that he seemed to be staring into the bar, toward France.

France laughed with a harsh nervousness. "It's really nothing," he said. "I have an idea that a minor employee has been embezzling from me. But there's no evidence. I'll handle it. Be seeing you again, Wentworth."

France swung about from the bar, and walked stiffly toward the main door of the club. His cane was in his hand—and he did not even pause to recover his hat from the check room!

For an instant, Wentworth hesitated beside the bar. His eyes followed the gray, stiffly held head of the steel man for a puzzled moment, switched off into the guest dining room, where he had been entertaining his fiancée, Nita van Sloan. It had been the strange sight of Carter France, chain drinking, that had pulled him from her side. His eyes sought hers now. He shook his head, motioned her to wait—and strode off after Carter France!

IT WASN'T strange that Wentworth should take an interest in France. Quite aside from a personal liking for the man, Wentworth had a deep interest in anything that verged on criminal menace. He might be wrong, but that request for Kirkpatrick certainly pointed toward criminal activity. Moreover, it was strange that the sight of an ordinary patrolman on the pavement could terrify Carter France!

Wentworth's firm lips were set in determination as he moved swiftly toward the street in France's wake. His was no idle curiosity. Whenever crime lifted its head to menace humanity, Richard Wentworth had a positive and active interest. It was an interest that more than once had brought him in imminent peril of his life; that led him to roam the night in a masquerade that would conceal his identity—and bring terror to evil-doers! For Richard Wentworth was secretly that lone wolf of justice whom all the Underworld feared—the Spider!

When Wentworth reached the door, he was just in time to see Carter France sprint into the street. The middle aged steel magnate flung himself at a passing Fifth Avenue bus, swung to the rear platform and began rapidly climbing the stairs! Yet Carter France's private car was parked at the curb! Wentworth had seen it there on his arrival at the club an hour before!

With crisp strides, he crossed the pavement, sprang into a taxi.

"Keep close to that bus," he ordered the driver.

Wentworth kept his eyes fixed on Carter France. The man he followed had gone to the extreme front of the double-deck bus, and sat hunched forward on a seat alone on the upper deck. His head twisted from side to side; he peered back over his shoulder and Wentworth caught the pale mask of his face.

Between Wentworth's brows, there was a knife-crease of a frown. Carter France was one of the most courageous men he knew, both morally and physically. He was cool and unshaken in crisis. Yet there was only one explanation of his conduct. He was in the throes of panic terror! And apparently the sight of a policeman had touched it off! An ordinary harness cop!

Wentworth leaned forward. "I'll board that bus ahead," he told the taxi driver quietly, and held out a bill. "Just keep the change."

Once on the rear platform of the bus, Wentworth hesitated a moment before climbing the stairs. He didn't want France to observe him, and yet he had to keep the man under observation. While he still waited, the bus slowed to a halt at a red light, and he heard France's voice lifted in a hoarse shout!

With a bound, Wentworth went up the stairway. He reached the head of the steps and a cry rose to his lips. Carter France was standing on the front seat of the bus, waving his cane wildly in the air. He was shouting down at the people in the streets, shouting as a man completely demented!

"Fools!" he cried. "Why don't you open your eyes! There's death all around you! Spies are eating the heart out of your country, and you pay no attention! They will stop at nothing! They kill helpless women! They rule the police! They drive men mad to get their secrets! Fools!"

THE BUS lurched forward at the change of the light, and Wentworth raced silently along the aisle. France twisted about, still shouting down at the pedestrians. He saw Wentworth, and a scream strained his throat.

"No, no!" he shrieked. "You shall not...."

He stepped toward the front guard rail of the bus, but Wentworth was upon him. He caught France around the waist from behind.

"Steady, man!" he called soothingly. "It's Wentworth! Take it easy!"

France flailed at him with the cane. The blows thudded against his thigh and hip. France screamed like a madman.

"Let me go, damn you!" he shouted. "You're a slave of the Master! Let me go!

Wentworth lifted France down from the railing, set his feet on the floor. He heard the conductor of the bus yell behind him.

"I'm your friend," Wentworth said quietly. "Take it easy, France. You'll be all right now!"

France wrenched free of his restraining arms. When he whirled, he had jerked his cane apart… and a sliver of deadly steel darted toward Wentworth's chest!

Wentworth cursed in amazement, dodged aside as he slapped the blade with the palm of his hand. The lunge went through the side of his coat within a fraction of an inch of his flesh! Instantly, Wentworth clamped his arm down hard on the blade, pivoted to his left. The sword snapped off short and France reeled back against the bus railing, staring at the broken fragment of his blade with dazed eyes.

Wentworth's voice was still cool. "Easy does it, France," he said. "You're not in danger now. Just take it…." His voice broke off, for with a despairing cry, France once more leaped to the seat. He flung the handle of the cane at Wentworth's head. Under a passing street light, Wentworth saw him clearly—*and it was the face of a maniac!*

Nevertheless, he hurled himself toward the man. His upflung arm knocked the handle of the sword aside, and he reached for France. He caught at him, and his hands snagged France's coat. He braced his body, pulled strongly… and the coat came free in his hands!

In the same moment, France leaped to the front railing of the bus! By some miracle of balance, he held his poise for an instant.

"You can't stop me!" he shouted. "I'll beat the Master!"

He dived, head-first, toward the street!

Wentworth cried out, lunged toward the railing. He heard the beginning of a scream. The bus lurched wildly as the left front wheel… lifted. It ground to a halt. There was no more screaming.

Wentworth looked down vacantly at the coat in his hand. He lifted his head and met the staring eyes of the bus conductor. The man began to move away from him with slow steps. His lips babbled sound that presently made words.

"I saw you!" The man gasped. "I saw you! You killed him!"

The conductor whirled and his feet clattered loudly on the steel steps. In the street, a woman screamed and a man's voice lifted hoarsely.

"There he is! On top of the bus! *The man who killed him!*"

CHAPTER 2
THE SPIDER WALKS

I T WAS horror which immobilized Richard Wentworth. He had seen Carter France go mad with terror and kill himself. But it was the things France had said which stirred him most deeply. To some they might seem mere mad maunderings. To the Spider, they had the ring of gospel truth. None knew better than he how swiftly and virulently the Underworld could strike!

Grimness settled about Wentworth's lips, turned the pleasant line of them into cold anger. His gray-blue eyes held the sheen of glacial ice. He scarcely noticed the crowd that swiftly gathered, or heard their accusing shouts. There was work to do—work for the Spider!

Even while Wentworth's thoughts canvassed the thing that had happened, he was in motion. He strode directly toward the

21

rear stair of the bus. He would not have much difficulty explaining to Commissioner Kirkpatrick what had happened, but he had no intention of being delayed at this time.

He went swiftly down the steps, and the conductor leaped down into the front ranks of the gathering crowd. He shouted accusations, thrust out a pointing finger at Wentworth.

"There's the man who did it!" he cried. "He threw him under the wheels of the bus!"

Wentworth did not seem to see the man, nor the crowd. He walked calmly across the platform, stepped down into the street. Men's red, shouting faces were thrust out at him. He walked toward the crowd, eyes fixed beyond them, a slight frown between his brows. Such was the force, the power of this man, that the people parted before him without an order. Men fell silent in his path, and squeezed out of his way, and he moved steadily toward the sidewalk.

Off near the corner, he heard the shrill clamor of a policeman's whistle. The cop's shout lifted hoarsely.

"Stop him!" he yelled. "Stop that man!"

Others picked up the cry. They were not the men whom Wentworth had passed at close range, but there were many others. They shouted… and the crowd surged toward where he stood, erect and confident, on the curb. France's coat was still in his hands; the broken sword blade still pinned through his clothing.

He turned toward a taxi at the curb, but the driver was not at the wheel. Wentworth's eyes skipped over the crowd, gauging its temper. One false move now would set them upon him like a pack of wolves. No traffic was moving in the street. Cars were jammed, bumper to bumper, across the width of Fifth Avenue. Farther away, horns were blaring in protest. Here, men leaned from their windows and shouted curses. There was no escape except on foot.

Wentworth pivoted like a soldier on his heels, and marched toward the policeman!

BEHIND HIS calm gaze, Wentworth's mind was working at lightning speed. He knew that he would have to move at once against the men who had driven France to his death. As soon as they heard about this, they would suspect that he had told all he knew about them. They would move, and fast. No, Wentworth could not delay for police red tape to unwind.

He moved toward the policeman, and the crowd closed in angrily behind him. But he did not seem to hurry, despite the pace at which his long easy stride covered ground. The policeman was only twenty feet away, only ten….

"A mistake here, officer," he said quietly to the uniformed man who stood with his gun in his fist. "I demand your protection against this mob."

His even tone, but more than that, the confident ease of the man, the calm assurance, stopped the angry words of the policeman. He looked beyond Wentworth at the crowd, and lifted his gun.

"Get along with you now!" he ordered. "The man has surrendered. Get along—"

Wentworth's leap was panther-swift. His fist connected solidly with the policeman's jaw. Before the man fell, Wentworth had his revolver. A long bound took him to the curb. His hand reached out, touched the roof of a stalled sedan… and a smooth vault placed him atop the car! Before the amazed and angry shout of the crowd could lift, Wentworth had leaped to a second and a third car top. People shouted in shrill fright inside the vehicles. Doors batted open and they spilled out into the street, but Wentworth raced on, as calm and sure-footed as a middle-distance hurdler.

Abruptly, his eyes narrowed. That was a Daimler there in the mouth of the cross street; a Daimler like his own! As he spotted it, the car wrenched out of the traffic and was driven up on to the sidewalk. He saw then the white turban of the driver and knew that the car was his! At the same instant, the door of the tonneau was flung open, and Nita van Sloan stood on the running board!

"This way, Dick!" she called clearly.

A half dozen long strides, and Wentworth bounded to the pavement. Nita jumped back inside, and he vaulted through the door. Instantly, the door slammed and his Sikh chauffeur, Ram Singh, sent the Daimler leaping forward! People scattered from the sidewalk. The horn blared. Wentworth opened the window of the car, ejected the bullets from the cop's revolver and, swiftly wiping it clean of fingerprints, tossed it out into the street.

"France killed himself," he said, his voice flat. "You should have remained at the club, Nita. The best thing you can do now is to take a taxi directly to police headquarters and explain to Kirkpatrick what happened."

Nita's smile was slow in coming, and there was concern in the depth of her violet eyes. "And you, Dick?" she asked softly.

Wentworth's lips drew grimly thin. He slid two fingers into his vest pocket, and drew out a slim platinum cigarette lighter. He needed to say nothing. Nita knew, as well as he, that the base of the lighter was used to imprint the deadly signature of… *the Spider!*

NITA'S FACE grew pale, and the smile pinched off the soft fullness of her lips. "It's as bad as that?" she whispered. Wentworth said slowly, "It's pretty bad, I'm afraid. You know France's reputation for courage as well as I. He was literally frightened into madness and suicide. Before he died, he shouted something about spies…."

Nita caught her breath, "And he has valuable patents! I mean, war patents! That new steel process!"

Wentworth nodded gravely. He was busy searching the dead man's coat pockets. He found nothing until his fingers slipped into the change pocket, then he frowned at the bit of torn pasteboard he held. He checked an oath. "What is it?" Nita asked anxiously. Wentworth shook his head incredulously. "Carter France, millionaire steel master," he said, "took a sightseeing trip on a bus tonight… to Chinatown!"

"Chinatown!" Nita gasped.

There was horror in her tones. To most people, Chinatown might be a place of artificial atmosphere, designed to mulct tourists. But she had seen the life that flowed beneath that surface. She had been trapped in its underground passageways, and she had heard the laughter of the East!

But Wentworth's face was impassive despite the fire in his gray-blue eyes. His voice took on the crisp accent of command.

"Nita, you will take a taxi at the next corner and go directly to Kirkpatrick. Be satisfied with nothing else. Ram Singh will presently pick you up at headquarters and take you to safety... to my home where you can be protected."

"And you, Dick!"

Wentworth shook his head. "You will tell Kirk in detail just what happened tonight. I can't afford to have the police looking tonight for... Richard Wentworth."

Nita's hand rested lightly on his arm, "Yes, Dick," she said. There wasn't a quaver in her voice, even though she knew he was walking deliberately into deadly peril. That was part of their life. The Spider was hated and hunted by the Underworld; in the eyes of the law which he supported he was a criminal—for his path led outside the rigid line of the law. Many times he had been judge, jury and executioner.

"Stop by that taxi, Ram Singh!" he called.

The big Daimler slewed to the curb, and Wentworth sprang out to assist Nita to the cab. For an instant, her eyes lifted to his. Her hand clung. Her smile was bright.

"Phone me, Dick... when you can," she said.

He squeezed her hand, then leaped into the Daimler. It surged forward under the thrust of its powerful motor. "The Bowery!" he called to the turbaned driver. "Stop short of Chatham Square, where it is dark!"

The Sikh turned his head for a brief instant, and the white gleam of his teeth showed through the thicket of his beard. *"Han, sahib!"* he cried eagerly. "Tonight, thy servant will have his chance to fight... even if it be only against yellow rats?"

Wentworth smiled faintly, recognizing the happy ring of a warrior race in Ram Singh's strong nasal voice. "It may be, my warrior," he said softly. "It may well be...."

His hand dropped to a hidden button and the left half of the seat slid smoothly forward, revolved to reveal a closely hung wardrobe, a brilliantly lighted mirror and make-up tray.

When presently the Daimler slowed for an instant where the black shadows of the elevated structure merged with the blacker shadows of tenement walls, the rear door opened and closed softly. The Daimler rolled on, but when it went under a street light the rear seat was empty!

THERE IN the shadows, was a figure that blended perfectly with the background. It moved without sound, drifted to the mouth of a crooked side-street and merged with the darkness. For a single instant, a feeble yellow ray of light from a dirty window brushed across that figure. It was a grotesque man, with queerly hunched shoulders, a long cape that swept to his heels. The face was shielded by the broad brim of a black hat, but the momentary flick of light showed a lipless gash of a mouth. Just a flash, and then the shadows swallowed him. But it was enough. The Spider walked this night.

It was a thin trail the Spider followed, and there was only his keen brain to tell him the importance of the lead he had picked up. Perhaps if he had not been alert for some such development, he might have missed the significance. But with half the world at war, the superior mechanical perfections of the United States' war developments were certain to be a target for spies and saboteurs. And they had struck their first blow terribly! Of that much, Wentworth was certain.

The clue pointed to Chinatown… and Carter France had been terrified at the sight of a uniformed policeman!

From the darkness where he lurked, Wentworth's keen gaze probed Haven Street. At the moment, there was no policeman in sight. The Spider waited… No one knew Chinatown better than he. By daylight, impatient trucks clattered their way through these narrow streets, and at night another hectic and artificial life held its brief sway—until the tourists left, and the blaze of garish signs was quenched. Then, Haven Street began its real life. It was not a life that a Westerner would recognize.

The shadows grew thick and murmurous. Men passed furtively in the darkness on silent feet, the sing-song nasal of their voices no more than a whisper. But it was the real life, the subterranean life that crawled beneath the streets and showed rarely on the surface.

In the darkness where he waited, Wentworth became abruptly tense. A policeman had turned the corner, his slow, steady footfalls making faint, rasping echoes. Wentworth drew the Spider's cape shroud-like about him. The cop's eyes stabbed the shadows uneasily. Once he checked and whirled swiftly to peer behind him.

Wentworth waited until the man was no more than a yard from the narrow doorway where he crouched, then he stepped boldly out. His cape swirled behind him; his twisted figure was menacing in the darkness. And the Spider laughed!

It was flat and mocking and ominous in the narrow street. It reached out, plucked at the taut nerves of the cop.

"Don't touch your gun, fool!" came the even, menacing cadence of the Spider's voice. *"The Spider speaks!"*

The policeman froze with his hand halfway to the gun beneath his coat flap. A strong shudder seemed to jerk all his muscles. His mouth was open, but no sound came from it save the rattle of his harsh breath.

"That's better, fool," the Spider whispered. "You have been false to your oath! For such as you, there is a penalty outside the law!"

The cop found hoarse words. "No, no," he whispered. "I couldn't help it. He made me do it. I tell you, *he made me do it!*"

The Spider moved toward him. His head lifted so that the dim light from the corner struck beneath the broad brim of his black hat. It revealed a face that in no way resembled the keenly intelligent, warm human face of Wentworth. The Spider's face was without mercy, cold, predatory, terrifying.

"You may live… on one condition," the Spider whispered. *"Take me to him—right now!"*

For a moment, terror turned the officer's lips gray. He stammered words that made no sense. Then cunningly drew a veil across his eyes. He said, eagerly, "You swear you won't harm me if I… if I take you to *him!*"

Wentworth's lips twisted in a thin smile. "If you try no treachery," he said, "I swear it!"

The policeman hesitated while fear warped his mouth, as

already it had twisted his soul. "No treachery," he whispered. "Follow me."

WENTWORTH STEPPED back into the shadows. His hand moved in an imperative gesture, then vanished into the blackness of his coat. "Lead on," his voice barely reached the policeman's ears. "I will be… *nearby!*"

The officer marched stiffly along echoing Haven Street, but Wentworth ducked immediately into the doorway behind him. He slid down a flight of wooden steps, into an echoing cellar. He leaned his shoulder against a packing case and it slid smoothly along the wall, revealing a narrow door. When he ducked through the opening, the packing case slid back into place.

There was only darkness here, dank and unventilated. Wentworth ran swiftly and presently, from another cellar, he climbed swiftly into a sour hallway which had a door opened to the street. He was there before the policeman had turned the corner of Haven Street. Wentworth was under no illusions about the policeman. The slyness of his eyes had betrayed his obvious purpose of leading Wentworth into a trap. But that was all the Spider desired!

He peered out from the shadows, and saw the policeman cross the street toward where an old Chinese sat before a curio shop. A pipe was between his withered lips. His eyes were closed as if he slept in peace.

Wentworth let his glance slide along the crooked street, and checked an oath that sprang to his lips. Towering head high above the other Orientals who thronged the pavements, came the insolently striding figure of Ram Singh! His eyes stabbed arrogantly about him, and the small yellow men of China scuttled out of his path. Venomous glances brushed across the broad-shouldered, bearded Sikh. They only made him swagger. From the sash twisted about his narrow hips projected the brass hilts of two knives as heavy and long as short swords. Ram Singh had been promised a battle, and he had no intention of missing out on it!

Wentworth swung his eyes back to the policeman… and was just in time to see him step into the curio shop. The aged Chinese rose slowly to his feet, picked up his stool and doddered into the shop behind him. Afterward, the door swung shut, and the light within was snuffed out!

Ram Singh was almost abreast of Wentworth now. "The curio shop, Ram Singh," Wentworth whispered, using the man's native Punjabi. "Knock at the door. Knock long and loudly. There is probably a knife in the window you could use."

The check in the Sikh's stride was almost imperceptible. He swung to the curb and gazed insolently along the street before he crossed toward the curio shop!

Wentworth smiled faintly. How well he could rely on his brawny servant! Where the *sahib* led, so would follow the fighting Sikh!

WHILE RAM SINGH pounded on the door, Wentworth slid across the street—a drift of black shadow in the darkness. He vanished into a doorway and crept through into back courts, which he knew like the palm of his hand. The slattern fences offered no obstacle and in a moment he was looking at the back of the curio shop. It had no visible door. The single high window was barred with steel. Even the basement offered a solid brick wall to his scrutiny.

The angry sound of Ram Singh's hammering and shouted demand for entrance echoed dimly to his ears. He sped on into the next yard, where there was a basement entrance. It was no more than a muddy ditch whose covering doors had long since disintegrated. The Spider dived through the opening, cape ballooning out from his shoulders. His hands caught the overhead beam and he swung far out into darkness, landing as lightly as a cat... on a concrete floor!

Ram Singh's shouts came through more clearly from this point.

Wentworth slid out a small powerful flashlight from a pocket of the cape. The shielded beam cast only a thread of illumination, but his keen eyes followed it easily across the floor toward the inner wall of the basement. It was composed of ancient brick. But it would take an eternity to sound out that wall for the secret doorway it undoubtedly contained. Wentworth looked instead at the floor. It was scrupulously clean. There was not a trace of dust, but there was moisture.

The floor had been scrubbed, and most assiduously, around a stack of battered ash cans.

Wentworth did not disturb the cans. His light brushed across the wall and found the twisted end of a disused gas pipe. Overhead the broken, loose ends of wires dangled. To the Spider's swift brain, the solution was obvious. A touch of the wires to the pipe would undoubtedly open the door. But if he touched the wrong wire, or the wrong combination of wires, he might equally well set off a death trap!

It suited the Chinese sense of humor that a too-clever man should kill himself!

Wentworth's lips set thinly. He did not intend the risk to deter him, but he would take his own precautions. He reached across his shoulder, beneath the cape, and his fingers closed on a guardless hilt. He whipped his hand forward... and a yard of slim Toledo steel glimmered in the darkness!

He maneuvered around the cans until he was pressed flat against the wall, then he thrust the wires forward with the tip of his sword. It was a factor of the set-up that the wires could be reached only if a person stood directly in front of the pipe.

There was a fat green spark as the wires touched the pipe, and for an instant afterward, nothing happened. Then, with a hiss and a roar, a solid stream of brilliant blue flame gushed from the twisted muzzle. It stabbed out fifteen feet from the gas pipe—a blue rod of flame an inch across. Had it hit Wentworth, it would have eaten a hole through flesh and bone as if they were cheese-cloth! Even at a full two yards' distance, he was conscious of the intense blistering heat of that flame. It was not ordinary gas, it was something as hot as oxy-acetylene.

Through a long, throbbing moment, the lance of flame vibrated in the air. Then as suddenly as it began, it was cut off. Lights danced before the Spider's dazzled vision. The smell of heat was close.

WENTWORTH WAITED tensely, his ears tautly attuned. Even so, he almost missed the sound he sought, an oil-smooth whisper of movement. He swung out the sword point toward the wall—and the metal tip touched nothing! A secret door had opened! With a swift, lithe spring, he lunged through into darkness!

The sword, reaching ahead of him, rang sweetly against stone. He whirled back against that wall and waited—conscious of a faint whir of machinery. There was a slight rasping sound, and he knew that he was closed in. The door in the brick wall had glided shut once more.

Still he waited. His eyes strained wide against the darkness and he felt the muscles tighten behind his ears. The racket of Rain Singh's diversion came to him dimly—no other sound. But he knew that, somewhere in this warren of death, he must have touched off an alarm. Someone would come to make sure that the invader was destroyed.

He extended the sword at arm's length and began to feel out the corridor in which he believed himself to be. The roof was close overhead. The wall behind and across from him was of brick. To his left, his extended sword rasped faintly... on steel!

He stood motionless, waiting, the sword poised before him. Ram Singh's hammering had ceased, but suddenly a new sound rushed to his ears. It was closer, louder... Ram Singh's eager shout of battle! No words came through, but he knew the note of the brown man's voice. He was chanting the war song of his native Punjab hills, in a broken and exultant rhythm! Ram Singh was fighting!

Wentworth whirled away from the steel wall and lunged in the opposite direction from which the sounds of battle seemed to come. He took two strides and the antenna of his sword once more rang on steel! He choked back an oath. Brick walls on either side, before and behind him steel portcullises closing the corridor to form a trap. He knew, without exploration, that it would be impossible to gain access to the door by which he had entered. The mechanism would have locked it!

Wentworth sprang to the steel portcullis; found it a solid sheet of metal. There was a narrow gun-port, but it was sealed immovably from the other side. No, the killers who held sway would be in no hurry to come for him. They would take their time, dispose of Ram Singh, and kill the Spider at their leisure!

Even as the thought brushed across Wentworth's mind, he heard Ram Singh's chant rise to a higher note. It grew rapidly louder. Mechanically, Wentworth estimated that Ram Singh had destroyed or put to rout the first force loosed against him, and he, too, was rushing on… into a trap!

Ram Singh's voice lifted in an angry, baffled shout. A Punjabi curse ran harshly along the corridor, and was cut off in its midst.

After that, there was silence.

Slowly, Wentworth backed away from the portcullis. With a quick gesture he slid his sword back into the scabbard between his shoulders, and flipped twin heavy automatics into his palms.

Ram Singh was down. Now they would come for the Spider… a trapped and almost helpless Spider, armed with weapons which the steel shields enclosing him would easily foil.

His lips drew back from his teeth. In the darkness, he laughed. The flat, metallic laughter of the Spider beat back from the narrow walls of his cell. It seemed to mock him.

CHAPTER 3
DEATH BELOW

THE KILLERS did not keep him waiting long in his close-walled prison. Within seconds after Ram Singh's vaunting battle song had been silenced, Wentworth caught the whisper of felt-soled slippers beyond the barrier. Deliberately, he flicked on his flashlight and gazed into the concentrated beam through a space of seconds.

Then he heard the delicate rasp as the gun-port cover was slipped aside in the steel portcullis, and at the same instant, overhead light flared down brilliantly upon him! But thanks to his preparations the Spider's eyes were not dazzled. He was ready. He saw the muzzle of a machine gun thrust in through the gun-port!

He whipped up his left-hand automatic at arm's length before him, and looked along the barrel. It was a superlatively cool movement. The machine gun muzzle was pointed directly at him. At any moment, the Chinese who held it might open fire. And Wentworth had to make this one shot sure. Ordinarily, firing from the hip, he could take a chance on his target. But this time....

For a fleeting second, he aimed, then he squeezed the trigger of his heavy automatic! The concussion of the blast in that enclosed space beat upon him with physical violence. He staggered, and with a shout rising in his throat, hurled himself at the shield!

As he leaped, he saw a ruddy flare of explosive fire beyond the gun-port. The machine gun muzzle was hammered back out of sight, and there was a shrill, lifting scream! Wentworth's bullet had sped true! With that single, careful shot, he had plugged the muzzle of the machine gun, so that it had exploded on pressure of the trigger!

On the heels of that blast, Wentworth reached the steel wall and thrust his own gun into the port! Deliberately, he sprayed the corridor beyond from wall to wall! When his automatic was emptied, he thrust his second weapon against the port and once more poured out a stream of hot lead. His ears ached from the impact of the blasts. And through that fury of sound he caught the screaming terror of the Chinese. They were trapped, as they had intended to trap him!

His deft hands flicked out the emptied cartridge clips and snapped new ones in his twin automatics as he bent to peer briefly through the gun-port. Four powerful Mongols, naked to the waist, lay still upon the floor. Another tried to drag his smashed body feebly away. He shuddered convulsively and lay motionless along side his companions.

Wentworth held his automatics ready while his eyes combed the corridor beyond. In a wall socket, from which a dummy brick had been removed, he saw the glistening steel of a lever. Undoubtedly, it was the one which operated the steel portcullis!

For a long moment he studied the lever, then once more pointed an automatic through the gun-port. The lever must be depressed, and he was shooting upward at it. His only chance was to carom a bullet off the upper face of the socket, and bounce a series of bullets downward against the shining steel!

Two of the first four shots partly depressed the lever. The next three missed the exact angle necessary to move the steel bar. He swore softly, switched guns. Seconds were skipping past. There undoubtedly were more of the murderous Mongols in this death warren.

Five times, Wentworth squeezed off bullets. Then steel rang on steel. There was a violent wrench upon his automatic, and he recovered the weapon just in time. The portcullis shot upward into a ceiling socket. Concrete seemed to cover the slot… but he was free!

The Spider laughed softly—free to walk into another trap! THE WAY behind was still solidly closed with steel, the door through the brick wall was closed. There was no retreat, even if he had been so inclined! But Ram Singh was helpless somewhere ahead where the enemy was!

The Spider had replaced one of the used clips in his automatic. In the other, he carried two bullets. That was his full quota of cartridges. He had no more. Still, nine shots… in the Spider's guns… should account for nine enemies!

Abruptly, as he stalked forward, the lights blinked out in the corridor. Instantly, he sprang a full six feet ahead, and glued himself to the opposite wall. But there was no attack, only the tenseness of waiting silence.

Wentworth crept forward slowly—cautiously. Yards slipped beneath his feet, and yet nothing happened. There was no change in the even flooring, no change in the character of the walls. But the place he sought could not be much farther. He must have passed completely through the basement beneath the curio shop. The sounds of battle could not have been far beyond this point.

Wentworth stopped, straining eyes and ears against the darkness. He heard a sound that would have meant nothing to most men—a faint, hidden metallic click. A smothered shout lifted into his throat, as he hurled himself frantically forward! Even as he leaped, the solid floor gave way beneath his feet!

By that fraction of a second, he had beaten the release of the trapdoor. The click had been the actuating of the mechanism! But quick as he was, Wentworth had not been able to gain much impetus for his leap. His feet had slipped on a yielding surface. He could see nothing ahead of him. His hands, clutching the two guns, stretched out before him frantically. Below him was blackness, and he was conscious of a fetid odor and a faint hissing noise. And Wentworth felt coldness race through him, while his body sailed through blackness. There was no question of what waited for him below! It was a den of snakes!

Brief as must have been that flight through space, he seemed to pass through an eternity. The cold forerunner of fear traced its way up his spine. He knew that already his feet were below the level of the floor on which he had walked. He had missed! He was falling, and….

A blow like the recoil of a six-inch gun kicked him in the chest! His guns flew from his hands. Even in that desperate moment, he heard them skittering away along the concrete floor. But they were of small importance right now. He knew that his body had struck the far side of the pit. Frantically, as he hit, he flung out his hands. His nails clawed at the roughness of the concrete. He wrenched his legs upward, sideways and his foot scraped the sidewall.

Slight as those contacts were, they saved him for the moment from sliding backward into the pit. The stench of it closed his nostrils. The hissing was louder, a hungry angry sound! Again he drove his feet frantically against the side wall. His nails caught in a crack of the concrete. He brought all the power of his marvelously trained body into play, as he wormed his way back over the brink, away from the pit.

His breathing was still paralyzed from the blow. He staggered to his feet, and leaned weakly against the wall. Behind him, there was another faint click, and he knew that the trapdoor had closed. But there must be a way out. He fought for balance, for clarity of thought. His head was swimming, and there was an aching hell of pain in his chest.

Reeling forward, he bent far over to comb the floor for his guns. It would be death to show a light. But what could he accomplish without his trusty guns? Desperately, he whipped out his flashlight, flicked it on. He tossed it to the floor and leaped aside. The beam laid a swathe along the concrete floor. But there was no glint of metal.

His guns were gone!

WENTWORTH STRAIGHTENED out of his crouch. His hand whipped over his shoulder to his sword hilt. He flicked the flashlight to him with the keen point, pinched out the light. Still no sound, only the waiting silence that mocked him. His killers were playing with him, with the cold, cruel patience of the East. Death traps were thick along his path. He was without arms, except for the slender needle of steel in his hand. If he survived the traps, *they* would be waiting!

The Spider sent his cold laughter bounding ahead of him. He gripped the sword in his fist—and charged!

He blundered into a right angle turn of the corridor, bounded away. Behind him, a heavy weight dropped with an impact that made the earth beneath him shudder. But his speed had saved him. Once more, flame stabbed blue-white and murderous from a valve... bored a hole down the middle of the corridor. But Wentworth had turned another corner.

He swept on. Silken curtains brushed across his face. He uttered a shout and leaped wide. Light blazed into his eyes. He whirled in a sharp, concentrated circle and his cold gaze swept the room into which he had plunged. It was hung with golden silk. There was a throne upon a raised dais at one end—a dragon throne. No one was in sight, and there was no sound... but in the middle of the floor lay the blood-stained body of Ram Singh....

A cry lifted into Wentworth's throat at sight of that stained, twisted turban. His friend and comrade was dead was his first flashing thought. But, even as the fury of grief rose to his throat he caught a flicker of an eyelid. It was no more than that, but it seemed that the movement was deliberate. Ram Singh was playing 'possum!

But Wentworth's shoulders sagged, and he pressed a palm heavily against his forehead. With leaden movements, he pulled his long cape from his shoulders and dropped it over the sturdy prostrate form of Ram Singh. He gripped his sword then, and looked about him with bitter rage. Nowhere did the silken curtained walls reveal a stir of life. But guns might be trained upon him through the drapes!

In the middle of that silk-hung room of death, the Spider stood with his single weapon, the spindle of steel. His broad shoulders were twisted, and his head thrust forward. He looked dangerous… and he was! But he showed no fear, no impatience. He knew this waiting game of the East. Presently, he shrugged and began the deliberate business of selecting and lighting a cigarette.

Behind him, a gun clicked against stone, but Wentworth never so much as turned his head. The men he knew were behind the drapes had been too silent before to make a false move now. It was an effort to frighten him—as well as an obvious indication of their intention to destroy him! Not many criminals dared to toy with the Spider as a cat would play with a doomed mouse!

Smoking his cigarette, Wentworth seemed the epitome of relaxed leisure, but behind the mask of his face, his brain worked furiously. Despite his mad race through the tunnel, and his several narrow escapes from death, he had not lost his sense of distance. He knew that he was in a sub-basement beneath the rear of the curio shop. There were two bowls of copper suspended from the ceiling which threw their indirect brilliance down upon him. On each side of the dais was a flaming censer of perfumed oil whose sickly sweetness cloyed the air.

From the corner of his eye he caught a swaying of the curtains and his lips smiled thinly. With his guns he could soon break this battle into the open. But if he had his guns, they would not have played the game this way!

IT WAS the Chinese who first grew impatient. Abruptly, there was a concerted rustling of the silken drapes. Through the arras, there stepped a full dozen of the half-naked Mongols armed with knives, hatchets, and automatics. And from behind the dais stepped a man fully seven feet tall. His hands rested upon a sword with a chin-high hilt!

Wentworth stood motionless in the middle of the room as the Mongols appeared. In the flick of an eyelash he snapped his cigarette full into the face of the nearest man… and leaped to the attack!

He charged the giant with the mighty sword with a charge so swift that only one of the Mongols found time to strike. The giant lifted his huge sword deliberately to attract his attention. But from the corner of an eye, Wentworth saw a hatchet man whip back his arm. With a whizzing sound the glittering, deadly axe hurtled straight at his head!

It was enough that Wentworth saw it. He ducked as he leaped for the dais and, beyond him, a man screamed terribly! The Mongol's hatchet had found a mark, but not the one intended! The blade buried itself to its haft in the breast of a comrade.

So much Wentworth saw as he sprang to the dais. His shoulder deliberately brushed the urn of perfumed oil and sent its liquid flame slashing across the gold carpeted floor.

Then he confronted the giant swordsman!

The man was braced to strike. His powerful naked arms swelled for the blow as his face contorted with fury. Even as

He charged the giant who
brandished the mighty sword!

Wentworth staggered and recovered from his planned collision with the tripod of the censer, the man struck! The blow was incredibly fast considering the weight of his weapon. It sliced downward at Wentworth's head!

The Spider did not hesitate. With the speed of his charge behind him, he went in under the down-sweeping shaft. He lunged to the side and suddenly, the needle of his rapier darted out. It was a two-edge blade and scalpel-keen. It slid in above the mighty arms and caressed the swordsman's throat.

There was no sound of contact but suddenly there was no control in the swordsman's arms, and his blade buried itself in the wood of the platform. A bubbling cry tore at his throat as he staggered forward, in slow, faltering steps that shook the floor. He pitched forward into the flaming oil.

But Wentworth had not waited for this. In an instant he struck; he went through the golden drapes. There was a narrow alleyway behind the silk, with no exit. That suited Wentworth. His outthrust hand checked him against the wall and he darted to the left. Behind him, the curtains bellied and steel clattered against the stone wall. Another hatchet had missed its goal!

The light came dimly through the sheer silk, made a half-gloom in the narrow alleyway. Out in the great throne room men were screaming and shouting hoarsely. Their voices lifted frantically in an ancient tong cry.

"*Shah! Shah!*" they keened. "Kill! Kill!"

Wentworth raced on but found no exit or break in the solid walls! Finally, he found the thing he sought. Prosaic in these exotic, murderous surroundings, it gleamed, common-place in the wall. An electric light switch! His hand swept across it.

He brushed aside the silks and leaped into the throne room which was lighted only by the spreading, flickering dance of the oil flames. The eerie light cast grotesque shadows on the walls, turned ruddy the half-naked bodies of the killers.

At the opposite end of the room from the throne, where the Mongols had thronged as he expected, Wentworth stood against a deeply shadowed wall. His voice rang out softly as he whispered, *"Ram Singh!"*

AFTERWARD, THE Spider laughed and leaped once more to the attack! As he sprang forward, the doughty Sikh surged up from the floor and cast aside the Spider's robe which had shielded him. Knives gleamed in his great fists. Together, side by side, they ranged into the startled killers, as the war chant of the mighty Ram Singh, lion among Sikhs, made a barbaric harmony under the hissing, deadly laughter of the Spider!

A yellow man wheeled, mad with fright, and flung up his automatic. Wentworth's slim needle of steel threaded death through his heart before he could fire. Twice more he lunged, and two more men were plunged screaming into eternal darkness. Once more Wentworth leaped, and he slipped on the deep-piled carpet. A hatchet man screamed in rage, whipped up his axe to bury it in Wentworth's un-fended skull. He poised the hatchet… and over Wentworth's head, there whined a glittering steel knife. It buried its sheen in the man's belly where the ribs parted, and brought quick death to the attacker.

Behind Wentworth, Ram Singh shouted his challenge. *"Wah,*

47

they are chickens that die easily!" he cried. "Such are not fit foemen for Ram Singh, mighty Sikh! I shall whip them with my honored steel!"

Wentworth was on his feet again, and the ranks of the killers seemed undiminished before him. They were trapped against stone walls. They gathered their forces, poised knife and hatchet, charged! Wentworth leaped to meet them, his sword a flicker of forked lightning. Where it struck, there was no need to strike again! But there were many of the enemy! So many….

In spite of his agile speed, Wentworth found himself driven slowly to the wall. His chest heaved with the violence of his efforts, and his blade dripped as he slashed and struck. The fire, which had created the diversion he needed, was an enemy now. Its weird flickering light afforded the enemy a target, and its heat forced them on like slave-whips. They could not retreat. They could come only forward… and meet the death of the Spider's sword.

They came, swarming, trampling their own wounded beneath slippered feet. And a sword can move only so fast!

The moment came when Wentworth's weapon, hard-driven, bit too deeply… and it snapped short to the hilt! An exultant shout went up from those who were near him.

Wentworth flung himself backward from the hacking stroke of a knife, flung his useless hilt into a man's face. He slipped… and went backward! Silks caught in his outflung hands and a curtain of gold ripped loose from its anchors to billow out over the charging killers.

That much Wentworth saw before the whirling curtain blotted out his vision. He rolled frantically aside, and then he heard the victorious lift of Ram Singh's chant! Joy rang in his voice.

"*Ha*, small squirming vermin!" he shouted. "Does thy throat pain thee? What of thy belly, pig! *Wah!* Thou hast no use for that heart of thine! I shall carve it out!"

Wentworth struggled to his feet, surged out from behind the curtains. He had rolled to one side of the battle, and there Ram Singh stood with his great trunks of legs solidly braced. He had caught up a hatchet with his left hand, and the great-bladed Khyber knife ran red in his right.

Wentworth's lungs were sobbing for air as they sucked in fumes from the fire. He coughed tearingly as he raced to attack again. He sprang to the dais and whipped the great two-handed sword from the platform's floor. He swung it on high… and sprang forward!

A moment, or an eternity, the battle lasted. Wentworth remembered the furious slash and parry, the hacking fury of the sword and Ram Singh's chanting joy. He knew that, presently, there were no more enemies standing, and he leaned, panting, upon the sword.

RAM SINGH stood on braced legs, and his clothing falling in ribbons from his mighty body. His bare chest heaved against the red gashes that had wounded it. There was blood in his beard.

"*Wah!*" he panted. "They are no more than mice! Scarcely worth a warrior's time!" He took a staggering step forward. "Yet it was a fairish sort of battle, *sahib!*"

He laughed and, laughing, plunged to the floor as a tree falls.

He struck heavily upon the men he had slain and lay without moving!

Swiftly, Wentworth bent over his comrade, pressing his wrist with hands that were swift and sure. The pulse was racing, thin. The Sikh had lost too much blood. Wentworth must lose no time in getting him to a hospital. But how to leave this doorless room, with a fire that crawled as viciously as writhing snakes across the floor?

Wentworth swore and stooped to heave the unconscious Sikh to his shoulders. It was a burden that would have floored most men, but the Spider's thews were whipcord and steel. He peered about him, drunken with fatigue, eyes burning with the hot fumes. No doors... but there must be openings. They would be controlled from the throne!

Grimly, Wentworth set his jaw. The spreading flames built a barrier across the room, mushrooming up to the ceiling. Each moment of delay made his task more difficult. Wentworth snatched up his cape and flung it across Ram Singh, pulling it close about his own face. Then he lumbered forward in a heavy trot with the great weight upon his shoulders. His run was a pitiful thing beside the Spider's usual flashing speed. As he reached the edge of the flames he hurled himself forward in a dragging leap.

He experienced a moment of intolerable heat as his flesh crinkled within his clothing. He staggered. Pain had its cruel way with his body and his lungs were stifled. But he could not pause to rest. He must go on. He groped toward the throne chair, his fingers pressing the scales upon the dragon necks that formed the arms. Nothing happened. He cursed, reeled to the other arm and Ram Singh's weight seemed to increase by the second. It was almost an accident that he depressed both of dragon's eyes together. He felt them yield, and for a long moment, he could not be sure that it was a door they had operated. But the flames were whipped by a sudden draft and the smoke began to move in a black veil across the throne room. There was a sullen roar in to the hot crackle of the fire.

Wentworth started a crazy laugh of relief as he choked on the fumes. Strangling, he wheeled toward the wall behind the throne, toward the split silk of the curtains which stirred faintly in the draft. He fumbled into his pocket for a brandy flask, bit at the cap as he fought his way on. Every step was a labor of Hercules. He went through the curtains and saw a dark oblong that he recognized, with a gasp of thankfulness, as a doorway.

Behind that wall, he would be safe for a moment, could doctor Ram Singh back to a semblance of strength with the brandy he held ready. He reeled through the door, got his shoulders against the wall preparatory to easing his burden to the floor. He heard the door rasp shut again behind him—and a flash of light blinded him.

Across the width of the room, braced against the wall, was a policeman. There was a gun in his hand, and it was pointed unwaveringly at Wentworth's breast!

The policeman opened his mouth almost mechanically, and when he spoke it was in the dead level of a somnambulist.

"I kill whoever enters here," he said thickly. "You are first!"

CHAPTER 4
MURDER TRAP

STARING INTO the steadily lifting gun of the police-man, Wentworth knew for once a feeling of utter helpless-ness. Even without the weight of Ram Singh upon his shoulders, he could not leap across the room in time to stop that inevitable bullet. He had not the strength! Nor was there any chance to talk the man out of his determination to kill. The symptoms were obvious. He had been hypnotized and ordered to kill!

Wentworth's eyes flew desperately about the room in which he found himself. It was small, luxuriously furnished in a combi-nation of East and West. Behind the policeman, a safe stood open and papers were scattered on the floor. There was no loose rug he might hope to jerk out from under the man, no chair he could grasp and throw. He would be shot before he could hurl his brandy flask at the man, unless....

Wentworth's gaze fixed itself on an electric fan just above the door, tracing the wires to the switch that was within reach of his outstretched arm. He shook his head sharply.

The policeman's gun was lifted completely now. His sleep-walker's eyes peered along the barrel; his finger already taut on the trigger!

"Wait, fool!" Wentworth snapped, and he made his voice harsh and commanding, as only the Spider could. "Wait, fool, would you kill your master? You cannot kill your master!"

The man's eyes widened under the probe of the Spider's mighty will. His finger wavered on the trigger.

"You…" he began hesitantly.

"Repeat your orders, fool!" Wentworth ordered. "What did the master… what did *I* command?"

The policeman moved his lips without sound, forming words in his throat, and while he hesitated, Wentworth reached out calmly and turned on the electric fan. It whipped into instantaneous speed. Its motor made a faint somnolent humming, and the blades caught the reflected lights. The policeman's head swung about uncontrollably toward this new distraction of his mono-rail thoughts… and Wentworth threw the brandy!

Not at the policeman. It would have done no good. There was no force in the flask and Wentworth could not move quickly enough to take advantage of a minor distraction. The policeman's vision must be momentarily blotted out! Wentworth flipped the brandy upward, into the path of the fan! The liquor was instantly diffused into a spray and hurled directly into the staring eyes of the policeman.

At the same instant, Wentworth slumped to the floor, eased his burden from his shoulders. The policeman cried out in pain. The gun hammered and racketed in the narrow room. The bullets smashed through the whirling blades of the fan, and the punctured metal began to shriek like an anguished animal. But Wentworth, free now of the weight upon his shoulders, leaped to the attack. One solidly planted blow stretched his assailant unconscious upon the floor!

Wentworth paused only to take the man's gun, then doubled back to Ram Singh and, slowly, poured remnants of the brandy down his throat. The Sikh strangled, stirred weakly.

"Wah, sahib," he whispered hoarsely, "Ram Singh is no warrior, but a woman of the lowlands. Without heart."

A faint smile stirred Wentworth's lips. The Sikh had slain his half score of men this night, with no other weapon than a knife and the strength of his arms!

"Thou art a man of mighty valor, my warrior," Wentworth told him in the strong nasals of Punjabi. "We have conquered. Rest you there."

Wentworth moved alertly across the room. Smoke was squeezing in little puffs beneath the closed door of the throne room. There was another exit, but he must move swiftly. The fire must be spreading up through the building. The police and the firemen would be coming soon—and there was no safety among their ranks for the Spider!

Rapidly, he knelt before the safe, ran through the papers. There was nothing of importance. They seemed to consist entirely of payrolls in which numbers, instead of names, were used, and in an inventory of the stock in the curio shop upstairs. Apparently, all papers of importance already had been removed! Wentworth straightened stiffly, turned toward Ram Singh… and it was then he saw a single small slip of paper on the floor before the exit. He snatched it up and frowned over the four ideographs he saw.

But there was no time now to decipher them. He tucked the slip of paper into his pocket, wheeled about. Ram Singh had staggered to his feet and leaned against the wall. The policeman was still unconscious.

"We'll have to carry him out, Ram Singh," he said curtly. "But meantime...."

Wentworth's fingers slid to his vest pocket and plucked out a slim cigarette lighter. He thumbed open the base, and pressed it against the door of the throne room. The door burned to the touch and he could feel the pressure of super-heat beyond. He had left a warning on the door, an ominous message that glowed there like fire, a sprawling thing of hairy legs and poison fangs— *the seal of the Spider!*

IT WAS an incredibly difficult road they took, with the burden of the policeman swinging between them. They followed tunnels where the heat of the fire faded slowly. The dim whine of sirens seeped through from above coupled with the shouts of men. But Wentworth knew his directions and, presently, they emerged in the basement through which he had first entered the den of the Master, humanity's newest menace.

They left the unconscious policeman in the court behind the adjoining building, made a swift and silent dash to the car which Ram Singh had parked. Wentworth put Ram Singh in the back while he jumped behind the wheel and guided the car swiftly, stealthily away from the danger zone. He drove without conscious effort, and his thoughts raced over the thing that had happened.

His invasion of the headquarters of the Master had accomplished something. He had destroyed the hideout, swept from existence a group of underlings... but he knew that the commander himself had escaped. Otherwise, there would have been no trap waiting for him in the room behind the throne.

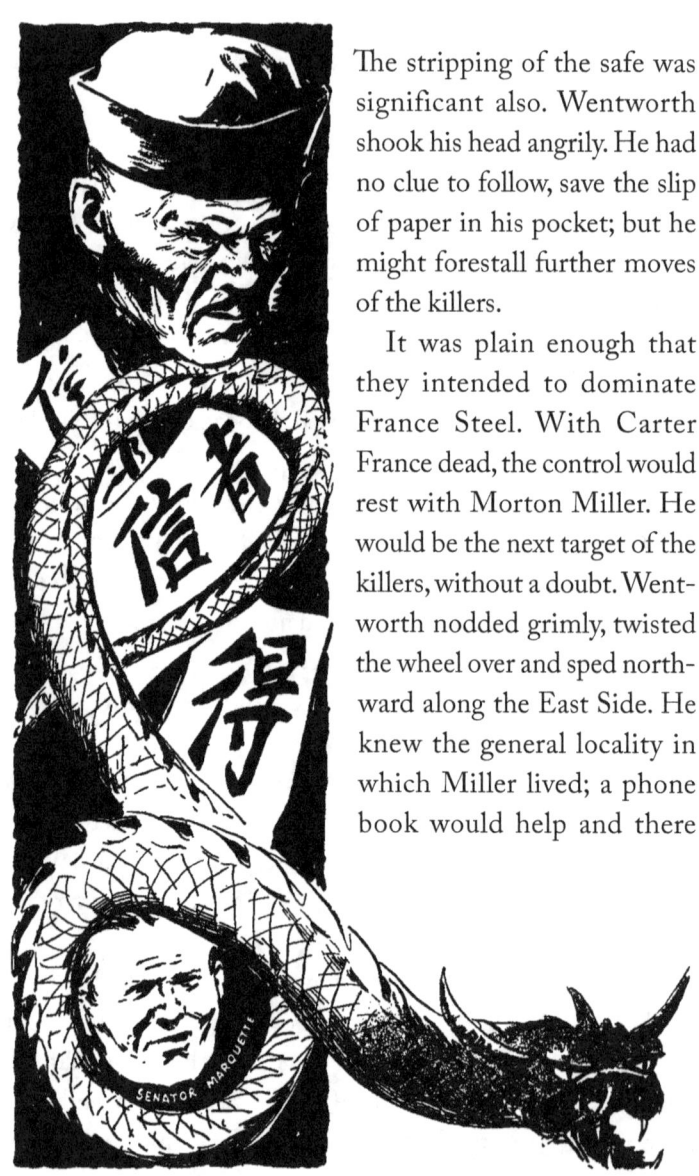

SENATOR MARQUETTE

The stripping of the safe was significant also. Wentworth shook his head angrily. He had no clue to follow, save the slip of paper in his pocket; but he might forestall further moves of the killers.

It was plain enough that they intended to dominate France Steel. With Carter France dead, the control would rest with Morton Miller. He would be the next target of the killers, without a doubt. Wentworth nodded grimly, twisted the wheel over and sped northward along the East Side. He knew the general locality in which Miller lived; a phone book would help and there was fresh clothing in the back of the car. He would lose no time.

Wentworth left Ram Singh at the home of his physician and took a taxi to Morton Miller's. He noticed that it was only a little after eleven o'clock. His fatigue was intense, but there was no opportunity yet for rest. He knew so pitifully little of this new peril to humanity. But he pieced together the fragments that were at his disposal: A man called the Master had the police force—or at least a portion of it—under his domination. This fiend, whoever

he was, had driven Carter France to kill himself. And France was no weakling!

Consequently, Morton Miller was in deadly peril, and Wentworth must warn him.

MILLER LIVED in a private house which stood on an exclusive block in the East Sixties. As Wentworth mounted the steps he saw a light on the second floor. He had resumed his own identity to make this call, and stood, leaning with an effect of casualness upon his ebony cane as he waited for the butler to answer his ring. But actually, Wentworth was taut with the need for haste.

The street was deserted and encased in the well regulated silence found in that part of town. Miller's house was only a few doors from Fifth Avenue where the traffic whirled northward in a never-ceasing stream. But within the house, there was no sound, and no movement that he could detect.

Wentworth swore under his breath, pressed the bell more imperatively. He could hear the dim whirring of the buzzer within the depths of the house. The light continued to burn on the second floor. There was no other sign of life.

Good lord! Could it be possible that he already was too late!

He stepped close and rattled out a sharp summons on the door with the head of his cane. The knocking echoed across the width of the street. He saw a policeman turn the far corner, pacing toward him deliberately. Confound it; he had to get into the place quickly! If he had to force his way in, he could not afford to be spotted here by the policeman....

Wentworth jammed his thumb down hard on the bell. The

policeman was only two houses away when finally the lights flashed on in the lower hall, and footsteps moved toward the door. Not until then did Wentworth take his thumb off the bell button.

The door was jerked open and a man in formal dress glared out at Wentworth. "What the devil do you mean?" he snapped. "It ought to be plain that I don't want to be disturbed!"

Wentworth nodded easily, "It ought to be plain, from my persistence, that the visit is important!" he said. "You are Morton Miller? Good. I am Richard Wentworth."

Miller's truculence faded under the ease of Wentworth's manner, and the commanding presence of the man. He said, uncertainly "Wentworth? Yes, certainly. I've heard of you… But at this hour!"

The policeman was pacing past the steps now. He shot a quick, observant glance toward them. Miller stepped back. "Won't you come inside," he said. "If it really is important…."

Wentworth stepped in with every appearance of carelessness, but his eyes swept over the elaborate foyer.

"It is," he said quietly, "if your life is of any value. Did you know that Carter France went mad and killed himself tonight?"

Miller said, hoarsely. "Good God, no! How did it happen? Oh, I'll take your things. My man's night off."

Wentworth laid hat and cane and gloves on a hall table, and Miller led him to a second-floor study, which light Wentworth had seen from the street. His keen glance took in the entire room, the shelves of books, the wood paneling of the walls.

"Tell me about France," Miller said, his voice low. "I can't believe he would… kill himself!"

Wentworth nodded, "Unfortunately, there isn't much doubt about it," he said, and related how it had happened. He was weighing the man before him, speculating on his presence alone here in the house. It might presage an attack… by the Master!

He broke off his narration abruptly, "Is your servant an Oriental?" he asked. "Is this his regular night out?"

Miller stared at him stupidly a moment, the heavy planes of his face slackened in surprise. "Why… That's a damned funny thing to ask. He's a Jap, or something of the sort. No, this is an extra night I gave him."

Wentworth said softly, "Just as I thought. Miller, you, yourself, are in terrible danger! France was killed by international spies who want to seize control of France Steel. You are the next in command now!"

Miller laughed incredulously. "Really, Wentworth, you don't expect me to believe a melodramatic thing like that!"

Wentworth's smile was tight. "War is melodramatic," he said, "and so was France's death. I advise you to phone the police for protection!"

Miller shook his head, smiling widely. "You've been reading the wrong kind of books, Mr. Wentworth!"

WENTWORTH'S ANGER was not at the insulting character of the words, but at the obtuseness of the man who refused to believe what was told him. He leaned forward and rested a hand for emphasis upon the desk, but before he could speak, the telephone bell whirred. Miller scooped it up, and he spoke in curt monosyllables of assent. Wentworth stepped slowly back from the desk, and once more his eyes swept the room. Was it possible that there was more than mere obtuseness to Miller's refusal to believe? Wentworth lifted a hand and casually unbuttoned his coat. Apparently, it was for the purpose of taking out his cigarette case.

Miller hung up and faced toward Wentworth. There was a grim tension in his face. Wentworth was lighting a cigarette. He nicked out the flame of his lighter.

"You lied to me, Miller," he said. "You are not alone in this house! The call came from an extension!"

"What? You're crazy!"

Wentworth smiled slightly. "I think not. It is possible to have a phone equipped with a buzzer, but all outside calls are rung by a machine. One second ring, two seconds pause, then another single ring and so on. That buzzer whirred steadily until you answered it!"

There was a high color on Miller's cheekbones. He said harshly, "Well, it's my business! I'll ask you to leave now!"

Wentworth shook his head slowly, "Not yet, I think. I could not hear words over the phone, but I caught the tone of the voice. I would take my oath that the man to whom you were talking is an Oriental!"

Miller came around the desk, striding choppily. "Get out, Wentworth!" he ordered. "What I do is my own business...."

"Not necessarily," Wentworth answered softly. "You could easily be attending to the Master's business! It seemed strange to me that France should be killed, when it would not help to

61

gain control over his company. Much better to intimidate him. It seems logical that he was killed—only because you already had sold out to the spies!"

Miller said impatiently, "I'm not interested in your theories. Kindly get out!"

Wentworth slipped two fingers into his vest pocket and pulled out the scrap of paper he had found in the room behind the Master's throne.

"Interesting bit, isn't it?" he drawled. "Or perhaps you don't read Chinese ideographs? There are just four characters, apparently repeating one of the analects of Confucius. The first radical means 'wise-man… or one-who-has-learned-much.' The second translates more simply. It means 'speech' or a 'big talk.' The third ideograph stands for 'one-who-rebels-against-his-master.'"

Miller was staring at the slip of the paper with widening eyes. Paleness crept into his cheeks. Wentworth, watching him closely, went on.

"The fourth ideograph can be translated a number of ways," he said softly. "Perhaps 'a fool's ravings' would be best. Or it might mean a lunatic. Shall I translate the whole thing for you? It means, 'To the wise man, the speech of one who rebels against his master is but as the ravings of a fool.' Which was Confucius' wise way of saying you shouldn't believe all you hear… especially if spoken by a traitor."

Miller appeared to wrench himself from a spell. "Damn you!" he said. "You've accused me of enough things! Now get out, before I throw you out!"

He hurled himself at Wentworth, who side-stepped easily.

But Miller did not check when he missed his opponent. He rushed to the bookshelves… whirled suddenly with a revolver in his fist! There was no anger in his face now, only a white determination to kill!

Wentworth knew in that instant that all the things he had half suspected about Miller were true! The man had sold out to the spies! Even as the thought flashed across Wentworth's brain, Miller squeezed the trigger of the revolver!

Wentworth flung himself wildly aside and the first bullet missed. He snatched a book from the shelf and hurled it at Miller's head. The man ducked, staggered back, and lifted the gun again! Wentworth swore harshly. He did not want to kill Miller. He had too much information that might be of value. Desperately, he dived at his legs. The gun crashed once more and Wentworth felt the bullet pluck at his coat as he drove his tackle home.

It was a savage tackle. He clamped his arms about Miller's legs and carried him along. Miller cursed as he brought the gun down on Wentworth's head, but the blow was weak. In Wentworth's grasp, Miller's body made a convulsive leap—and lay entirely motionless!

Wentworth leaped to his feet and stared down at the prostrate body of Morton Miller. The gun lay useless beneath his hand and his head rested on a dark sluggish pool! Wentworth bent sharply forward, and saw the reason! Miller had been driven against the fireplace. The brass, pointed knob of an andiron had penetrated his brain!

Wentworth was momentarily shaken by the unexpectedness

of the man's death. Then an implacable coldness brought a stern look to his face. The man had richly deserved his death, however much the Spider wanted to keep him alive for the moment. Moreover, his demise would block the plans of the Master for the present! Without this slave, the spies could not gain the secrets of France Steel!

Grimly, Wentworth drew out his cigarette lighter and bent to press its base against the dead man's forehead. The Master should know who had thwarted him! The seal of the Spider burned on the man's pallid flesh!

Wentworth turned to Miller's desk with swift efficiency. He found no records of any value, but there were papers in the center drawer which obviously were a series of chemical formulae! Miller had unquestionably planned to surrender important information to the spies!

WENTWORTH'S HAND stabbed to the telephone and jabbed the button at the base of the instrument. It would be simple to speak with Miller's voice, and order whoever had called him to the studio! Yes, much simpler than racing through the house to find the person! Wentworth jabbed the buzzer again, but there was no answer.

He swore and raced out of the study to start a swift search of the house. He found four extensions to the phone, but no other thing that might point to the whereabouts of the speaker. Wentworth doubled back to the studio, began carefully to wipe out any possible fingerprints. But he must waste no more precious time. The Master was temporarily checkmated, his force disrupted. Before he could organize again, Wentworth intended to strike!

He strode swiftly to the foyer, caught up his hat and cane—Then stopped, in amazement. There was only one glove!

He closed his eyes, swiftly reviewed his entrance, almost certain that he had placed both gloves on the table. Certainly, he had not carried one glove to the study with him! He could not afford to leave the matter in doubt. He had come here in his own identity tonight, carrying his own hand-tailored gloves. The Commissioner of Police, Stanley Kirkpatrick, would need only to glance at the missing glove to identify it as Wentworth's!

But a quick search of the study revealed no trace of it. Was it possible he had dropped it outside on the steps or walk? He ran down the steps again, with a growing suspicion in the back of his mind. He was certain now that he had left the glove on the table in the hall. The same man who had called Miller was the one who had his glove!

Wentworth's lips twisted in irony, and his eyes had a cold glint. He had come in friendship, had been forced to a kill. Now the whole thing had turned into a trap for the Spider! Had it not been for the seal upon Miller's forehead, he could remain here while he summoned the police. Dangerous as that was, it was better than fleeing to be identified by the missing glove!

But the Spider was not yet defeated. If his suspicions were right, the man who had stolen the glove was only waiting for him to leave before planting the article, and phoning the police!

Very well, he would give him his chance!

Wentworth noisily opened the front door, fingered the night

latch off, and stepped onto the stoop. Lest the man he suspected be watching he closed the door tightly and began a close search of the steps, the sidewalk and the gutter. But keen as were the Spider's eyes, he did not see the pale blur that showed for a moment at a window and then faded into darkness. Within the darkened room, a short man with narrowed black eyes ran swiftly toward the hall, and up the steps to the study. He tossed the glove beneath the desk, snatched up the phone.

"Hello!" he said hurriedly. "Police headquarters, quickly. I want to report a murder. A man named Richard Wentworth just killed Morton Miller at his home. He put the Spider seal on Miller's forehead. His glove is under the desk!"

The man answered a few swift questions as to the address, and whereabouts of the body; then he hung up on the further investigations of the police. He bounded across the room, pressed the edge of a wall panel and a secret door opened silently. He sprang inside, closed the door behind him.

On the sidewalk before the house, Wentworth straightened from his futile search. With two long bounds, he went up the steps, and closed his single gloved hand on the door knob. At that moment, faint with distance, he heard the wailing complaint of a police siren!

He swore sharply. This was full confirmation of his guess! The police were on the way—and his glove had undoubtedly been planted in the study! Wentworth smiled thinly, manipulated the latch on the door and stepped inside! The police would be here in less than a minute. There would be no time to escape, but he could recover his glove—and perhaps catch the man who had planted it!

Wentworth bounded up the steps on silent feet, sprang into the study—and stopped. He saw the glove at once beneath the desk, but the room itself was empty of life!

He shook his head with chagrin. Incredible that anyone could move through the house and yet remain invisible and inaudible to the Spider! Yet this glove was proof that it had been done! His eyes combed the bookcases, the wood paneling for any possible secret place. His lips made a thin line against his teeth. It was more important that he find a clue to the identity of this international criminal, who called himself the Master, than it was for the Spider to run from danger!

WENTWORTH'S GUN flipped into his hand, and he sprang toward the bookcases. It took him a matter of seconds only to determine that the bookcases were fastened securely and did not swing out. The wood paneling of the walls was an obvious place for a hidden door.

His sensitive fingers hastily ran over the panel edges, while the siren's shriek came closer. It wailed into silence still a couple of blocks away.

Abruptly, Wentworth uttered an exclamation of satisfaction. He had spotted a discrepancy. A bit of molding showed a dark, unwaxed line beside it… as if, in sliding sideways, it had faintly marked the wood! Wentworth tugged at the bit of molding—and the panel door swung open to his touch!

Instantly, his flashlight probed into the darkness. His automatic flipped to his fist. He peered cautiously inside. A narrow

67

flight of stairs led downward. At one point, there was a slight widening of the passageway, a seat with a telephone. But the passage itself was empty! Even as he stared, a door closed softly, and there was the sound of running feet on concrete!

He sprang back to the window, saw a small figure duck into the shadowed doorway of a house three doors down the street. At the same instant, the police car swept around the corner and raced toward the Miller mansion. Wentworth swiftly stepped back from the window. It was too late now to follow the fleeing man.

Wentworth stood in the middle of the study, heard the shriek of brakes as the police car skidded to a halt. He smiled abruptly. In two long strides, he was beside Miller's body. It was the work of instants to heave the man's bulk up from the floor and thrust it through the secret doorway. The andirons followed. He hastily kicked a throw rug over the blood spot on the floor. It would soak through in time, but for the present it was safe. He did not expect to remain long in the house of Morton Miller!

But there were other things to be done. Wentworth grabbed up Miller's waste-basket, jammed with paper. He set it inside the secret passage and touched a match to it before he closed the door.

Hastily, he crouched before a mirror, and began to touch up his face and hair with make-up from a small leather kit from an inner pocket. While he worked with one hand, he reached for the telephone, spun out a number on the dial… a number so well known that his left fingers found the proper notches.

Below stairs the doorbell began to whir!

Wentworth was graying and roughening his eyebrows with skillful touch when the call went through. "No names," he said softly. "How are you, my dear?"

The sweet voice of Nita van Sloan came happily in his ear. "Oh, at last!" she cried. "I have been worried. Things have been happening!"

"There?" Wentworth snapped.

"Oh, no," Nita laughed. "There's been a fire in Chinatown…."

Wentworth smiled grimly as he turned his attention to changing the line of his mouth. It was fortunate for him that Nita worked for, and not against, him! She knew too much of his methods.

"I promised to call you, dear," he said. "I have to go to Washington right away, and I didn't want you to be alarmed. Morton Miller is dead, as well as France. Miller had sold out to the spies. Leader calls himself the Master! Have to have government help."

Nita said, somberly, "Dick, I hear someone hammering on a door! I can hear it even over the telephone!"

Wentworth laughed lightly, "Yes, the police are paying me a call, but there are still a few seconds before they become too impatient. Can you figure, dear, why Miller should grow pale at my translation of four Chinese ideographs. 'To the wise man, the speech of one who rebels against his master is but as the ravings of a fool.' Yes, I know it doesn't seem to make sense, but neither is there any apparent reason why the Master should have taken it from his safe among important papers. It was certainly dropped by accident."

Nita said, slowly, "Dick, that ideograph that means 'ravings of a fool.' Doesn't it mean a madman, too? A lunatic?"

Wentworth said sharply, "Yes! Of course!"

"France went mad," Nita said. "A wise man is one who has learned much… Do you think it could be a threat?"

The hammering of the police was insistent now. A torch threw a white beam across the window.

"Thank you, my dear," Wentworth said softly. "As always, you are my inspiration! I'll see you before long! Morton Miller has to go down and let in the police!"

Nita said, "But Dick, you said… Oh, I understand now! You are… Morton Miller! Be careful, my love!"

Wentworth laughed, softly. *"Au 'voir, cherie!"* He put the phone back on its cradle, made the finishing touch to his makeup and started down to the foyer. He brushed an electric switch and turned on the light in the lower hall. His makeup was hurried, and he did not resemble Morton Miller very closely. But the police did not know Miller!

WENTWORTH STRODE to the door, whipped it open. "What the devil do you mean, making all this…" He broke off. "The police! What in the world do you want?"

One of the policemen had his gun ready. He pointed it, not very positively, toward Wentworth.

"We got a call there was a murder in this house," he said harshly. "How come you took so long answering the door?"

Wentworth answered indignantly. "It is my home! It is my privilege to answer the door when I like, or not at all! As a matter of fact, I didn't care to be disturbed. There has been no murder committed here!"

The officer's gun was sagging. "Well, maybe so," he said. "But we gotta check up anyway. The phone call said the body was in the study."

"Nonsense!" Wentworth exploded. "However, you may come up and make your inspection. I realize you have your duty to perform. Right this way!"

He gestured to the officer. The man entered apologetically, and the other policeman followed more warily.

As they went past him, he struck twice. The two men slumped to the floor, unconscious.

Instantly, Wentworth snatched a hat from one of the men, clapped it on his head and darted for the door. He had his own hat, gloves and cane thrust inside his coat. The police car stood at the curb. He had the key in his hand….

CHAPTER 5
A FOOL BABBLES

WENTWORTH ABANDONED the confiscated police car at the first opportunity, walked two blocks to a subway which sent him hurtling downtown. By this time, the smoke of the wastebasket fire should have revealed the whereabouts of the corpse—and destroyed the chemical formulae that Miller had been writing for the spies!

Also, the police would have broadcast Wentworth's description, and disguise!

Wentworth stood on a deserted platform of the train and swiftly removed the last traces of make-up. When he left the subway, he was Richard Wentworth once more, lithe, commanding, with proud head carried high, and jauntily swinging a cane.

A taxi sped him toward the river to the amphibian which was kept at one of the piers.

The cab jerked to a halt at the waterfront—and a curse sprang to Wentworth's lips! Clearly enough in the stillness of midnight, he could hear the throttled roar of his plane's engine! Someone was warming it up for a takeoff, yet he had issued no orders!

Flinging the money at the driver he raced into the pier house. His hand flicked to the gun beneath his arm, and he lunged in the direction of the panel of orange light which shone upon the black heaving waters. The plane rode easily on the breast of the river, and Wentworth could see a man in the cockpit!

He bounded through the door to the ramp, whipped out his automatic, as a woman's voice spoke quietly just at his elbow.

"It's all right, Dick," she said. "Jackson is just warming up the plane for you. I knew you'd be using it."

Wentworth whipped about to look into the smiling face of Nita van Sloan. She wore a flying jacket and a helmet, and her round firm chin was set in determination.

"I'm going with you, Dick!" she announced flatly.

From the cockpit, Jackson waved a hand, cut the motors to idling speed and climbed out on the wing.

"All set, major!" he called, using the title he always gave Wentworth, for they had served together in the army where Jackson had been, as now, Wentworth's able sergeant.

Wentworth smiled slowly, stepped over to take Nita's arm. "I was thinking a little earlier tonight how fortunate it is that you are on my side! It will be an excellent idea for you to go with me, I think. You will be safer with me than alone in New York!"

Nita lifted the smooth arches of her brows. "Safer, Dick?" she asked, and her full lips curved mockingly.

Wentworth laughed. He knew that Nita was just as deeply concerned over the struggle into which both of them were embroiled. He knew that her fears for him gave her no rest… but as always, she showed him only a brave and smiling face.

Wentworth plunged into the flying jacket Jackson offered, caught up the helmet and flung out swift instruction. He told the sergeant about Ram Singh and the struggle in Chinatown.

"Keep Ram Singh undercover until his wounds are healed," he ordered briefly. "See Commissioner Kirkpatrick and tell him I've gone to Washington, and that a big gang of international spies is operating in New York City. They are using Orientals, but I doubt that they are working in the interests of any single country. Consequently they are more dangerous. It was one of their headquarters that burned in Chinatown tonight. I believe their attacks at present are centering on France Steel."

Jackson saluted briskly, "Yes, major."

Wentworth smiled into the man's broadly honest face. "And take good care of yourself, Jackson," he said. "I have good reason to think that these spies have spotted me as… another gentleman whom they fear!"

Jackson's face grew stern. "I hope they give me a chance, sir. Am I to tell the Commissioner how you're traveling if he asks?"

Wentworth hesitated. So far as he knew there was no alarm out for him. The police had seen him only in disguise.... But he had no way of knowing what the spy hidden in Miller's house had phoned the police!

"On second thought," he said slowly, "you will tell the Commissioner that you do not know where I am! Otherwise, give him the full story."

Jackson saluted again, and Wentworth gave Nita a hand along the wing. Jackson threw off the last line, and Wentworth taxied the amphibian out of the slip onto the breast of the river. Brooklyn Bridge was behind him, and ahead was the straight broad stretch of water to Governor's Island. He spotted a ferry trundling across the East River, calculated its pace and cracked the throttle. A take-off in the darkness was not too difficult if he did not hit some unseen snag. That was a risk he must take....

THE TAKE-OFF was uneventful though startled eyes turned toward them from the ferry, and Wentworth swung in a wide circle to the southwest, closing the cockpit cover. Instantly, the soundproofed cabin cut out engine sound and Wentworth turned to smile at Nita. Her eyes were grave.

"Is Washington threatened?" she asked quietly.

Wentworth held his smile. "I know of no threat as yet," he said. "I'm going to try to convince the Federal Bureau of Investigation that an international gang is operating. Where the interests of the country are so viciously threatened I cannot risk failure to notify them. Also, there is a senator, Marquette, from the west, who has been making repeated charges that the nation is riddled with espionage. I want to pool information with him."

Nita nodded quietly, leaned forward to switch on the radio, as she fitted a single earpiece over her head.

"You said that this was an international gang," she said. "Why do you say that when the headquarters are in Chinatown?"

Wentworth frowned. "It's deduction," he admitted. "But the Chinese could have no possible use for the secrets of the France Steel process. Miller's servant, one of the gang, was a Japanese. But while they might have use for the process, they would not care about controlling the American plant. Too difficult to get the finished product shipped home. And control over the plant seemed to be a chief concern of the criminals."

Nita nodded. "It sounds right to me. Also, there is the fact that France was openly ordered to Chinatown. That makes the Oriental operations seem like camouflage. I…." She broke off suddenly, and Wentworth realized that she was listening to something that came over the radio.

She motioned to him, and he slipped on his own headset. He was listening intently to the announcer:

"… *an amphibian, license NC 99897, last seen leaving New York in a southwesterly direction. All private airports requested to notify New York Police immediately on sighting this plane. Police of all cities, signal seventy-nine. Repeating…. "*

Nita's face was pale. "They mentioned you by name, Dick,"

she said, her voice held even by an effort. "It's a general order to pick you up for questioning. What is 'signal seventy-nine?'"

Wentworth frowned at the black sky before them, as he realized that the distant glow was the lights of Philadelphia. "Pick up suspect in crime of violence. Dangerous," Wentworth said slowly. "It's the interstate police code. They must have reached the hangar only a few moments after we took off. Kirkpatrick would know of the plane. The police have a listing of every one hangared within city limits."

Nita's hand reached out to rest lightly on his arm. "Then… someone saw you at Miller's!"

Wentworth did not answer, but his lips drew into a thin bitter line. It was the old story over again. In fighting the battle of humanity, he inevitably came in conflict with the law. And the law took his trail! But he would not, could not, turn aside on that account. The pursuit would make his task more difficult; it could not stop him.

"I've flown you into danger, dear," he said quietly. "We'll have to set the plane down outside of Washington. Then you'll head back for New York."

Nita shook her head, her lips as rebellious as the chestnut curls that escaped from beneath the helmet. "You need me more than ever now, Dick," she said with determination. "The report made no mention of me. I can interview the F.B.I. men. You would be arrested on sight!"

Wentworth looked at her and met her brave smile. He laughed softly. "My comrade at arms!" he said, and the words were a caress. Then he turned to the business of navigation.

THE SPIDER AND THE WAR EMPEROR

BECAUSE OF the necessity for caution against detection, it was afternoon when Wentworth and Nita drove into Washington in a rented car. He had managed to land the plane in a field surrounded by woods shortly after dawn.

Wentworth swerved the car to the curb near a drug store soon after they entered the city limits.

"Stay with the car," he told Nita briefly. "I'm going to try to get through to Senator Marquette by telephone."

"It's dangerous!" Nita urged.

Wentworth nodded carelessly as he stepped to the pavement. "It isn't that I doubt you, dear, but the senator has a reputation for being extraordinarily diffident with women. He has had a male secretary during his entire twenty years in the Senate."

Wentworth's eyes stabbed sharply about him as he crossed the pavement to the drug store. He had taken the precaution to disguise both his appearance and Nita's. Still, it was better to be cautious.

There was no trouble in getting through the senator's office. The secretary's voice came crisply over the phone. "I'm sorry, sir. Senator Marquette has left for the Chamber. It's possible I can overtake him, if it's important."

"Vitally important," Wentworth said quietly. "I have information to give him concerning the investigations he has been making on espionage."

"Just hold the wire, sir," the man said, then the wire was silent. Wentworth waited tensely in the phone booth, as a frown cut a knife crease between his brows. It was unusual, to say the least, that the secretary should have offered to go for the senator before he had even learned the nature of the call. Moreover, the secretary had not even asked his name! Wentworth's gray-blue eyes narrowed sharply. He might be mistaken, but he could swear he heard a furtive click on the wire… as if a wire-tap circuit had been opened or closed!

A sudden thought sent a startled exclamation to Wentworth's lips. It was fantastic, but this was precisely the sort of trap Kirkpatrick might be expected to suggest. He would easily couple the message sent by Jackson with the fact that Wentworth's plane had sped southward, and that Senator Marquette also was interested in the suppression of espionage! Yes, Kirkpatrick would be sure Wentworth would get in touch with Marquette! It was pure deduction, but Wentworth was positive he was right. He glanced sharply out through the glass door of the phone booth.

A half dozen people were eating at the soda fountain and other customers stood at the drug counter. Near him was a man looking over the titles of some bargain books in a rack. None of them seemed interested in Wentworth. Abruptly, he made up his mind.

Fumbling in his wallet he fingered out a ten dollar bill which he allowed to flutter to the floor inside the booth. Then he replaced the receiver, opened the door and stepped out. As he had expected, the man at the book counter glanced toward him and the booth. He saw the man's eyes widen and knew he had seen the ten dollar bill!

Wentworth hurried toward the lunch counter, climbed on a stool and ordered a soda. In the mirror, he watched the man at the book counter. His glance followed Wentworth covertly, then he stepped inside the booth and closed the door. He made an elaborate business of putting through a number, dropped a coin… Wentworth smiled faintly. His head jerked suddenly toward the door. A police radio car, racing with silent siren, skidded to a halt at the curb. Both occupants bounced out, guns ready!

WENTWORTH'S LIDS drooped over his eyes. Once more, his keen deductions had snatched him from the maw of danger! It had been necessary to make sure he was right. Now he knew that Senator Marquette was watched; and could take further precautions. But he was not yet safe! The police lunged into the drug store, darted directly toward the phone booth. A woman uttered a choked scream.

"Don't worry," one of the officer said. "It's just a pinch."

They converged on the booth, and Wentworth slid from his stool, as everyone else had done, taking his soda with him.

"I'm getting out of here before the shooting starts," he muttered to the man beside him.

"Me, too!" the man snapped, bolting for the side door.

Wentworth moved toward the front entrance and others started in the same direction. He would have to be ready to make a run for it. As soon as the police nabbed the man, he would explain, point Wentworth out… But Wentworth had no intention of letting the man get into trouble on his account!

At the entrance he stopped. Nita was on the running board of the car, and he motioned her behind the wheel. She nodded quickly, and there was a puff of smoke from the exhaust. The

The crash of the shot was like a
thunderclap in the Senate.

police were sneaking up on the phone booth. Abruptly, one of
them yanked open the door, jammed his gun inside.

"Hands up!" he snapped. "Don't try nothing. We got you
cold!"

The man yelped in surprise, squeezed out of the booth. "I

didn't do nothing!" he cried. "I was just phoning my wife! Look, I'm still connected!"

"You was like fun!" the policeman rasped. "Put out your wrists."

"Oh, officer," Wentworth called easily. "The man is telling the truth. I am the man who called the senator!"

One of the cops wheeled about, and Wentworth whipped up the soda which he still carried in his hand. His aim was perfection. Liquid and ice cream flew from the glass and caught the surprised policeman fairly in the face. He reeled back against his companion, collided with the book counter. There was a deluge of volumes, a muffled yelp and angry curses.

Wentworth lifted his voice once more, "You may keep the ten dollars for your trouble, my man!"

He set the empty soda glass down upon the counter and went across the sidewalk with every appearance of leisure. Nevertheless, he required only two bounds to reach the running board of the rented sedan. Nita whirled it away from the curb, and stepped on the gas.

Wentworth settled into the seat, and his smile was grim. "Kirkpatrick figured out my next move, and had the police waiting for me," he said. "The senator is guarded. His phone is tapped."

Nita said indignantly, "Stanley Kirkpatrick should be ashamed of himself! He knows you're only trying to help him!"

"Kirk would tell you," Wentworth said quietly, "that he doesn't want the help... of murderers!" He flicked on the radio, heard the first call from the police announcer launching the pursuit. But they had not spotted the license number of the car, and the description still presented a picture of Richard Wentworth—not of his disguise. Wentworth tuned the radio to a newscaster, caught him in the middle of a sentence.

"... and the galleries are jammed. There are many prominent figures of Washington life here. I see Justice Murdock of the Supreme Court. He is leaning over the railing, peering down into the floor of the Senate. And there's the wife of the President! There is always a crowd when the Lion of Wisconigan makes a speech, but even he has never had such a crowd as this! Many of the Congressmen are on the floor, also."

Wentworth frowned. "That's Marquette he's talking about

now. If he's going to make a speech, it may be some time before I can get in touch with him."

"… benefit of those who tuned in late," the announcer went on, "we are about to broadcast the speech of Senator Marquette from the floor of the Senate. The Senator phoned the studios a short while ago and announced that he would expose, on the floor of the Senate, the greatest espionage ring ever to operate in this country. Senator Marquette has secret sources of information, he says, and has learned much about the operations of foreign spies.…"

Wentworth choked down a sharp oath. "One who has learned much…. Good Lord, Nita! Now I understand that message in ideographs, and why the Master intended to carry it away with him! It was a threat against Senator Marquette!"

NITA TURNED a quick, alarmed face. "One-who-has-learned-much was the first ideograph," she said. "The second was *speech*…. The third, 'rebels-against-his-master.' Oh, Dick!"

"Exactly!" Wentworth said harshly. "The fourth ideograph tells the fate which faces Senator Marquette if he goes through with this speech! The same thing that happened to France! *The Master intends to drive Senator Marquette insane!*"

Nita spun the car around a corner and moments later whipped into an avenue that cut across the concentric streets of Washington. Ahead of them, the dome of the Capitol lifted above the greenery of trees. The car crashed through a changing light, and Nita drove down on the accelerator. No need for Wentworth to tell her his plans. She knew. Somehow, in spite of the police guard, Dick would get through to save Senator Marquette.

"This means," Wentworth said softly, "that Marquette really has something important. There's only one way to work this, Nita. I'll have to kidnap him!"

Nita nodded as quietly as if he had announced that he was hungry. She did not even consider the difficulties before him. After all, Richard Wentworth was the Spider—and those who knew, called *him* the Master of Men!

"What shall I do?" she asked.

Wentworth shook his head. "Just park where you can drive close to the portico on the northeast, nearest the Senate chamber. You'll know what to do when you see me."

The announcer's voice was confidentially low. "Senator Marquette has just entered the Senate Chamber. That applause you hear comes from the floor as well as from the balconies. His secretary, Roger Stickney, has a thick brief-case in his hand. The Senator is taking it from him and placing it on his desk. He will not speak there, but from the rostrum before the chair of the president of the Senate who is, as you know, the Vice-President of the United States. The microphone is ready for him. The Senator is not smiling as usual. His face looks very stern...."

Wentworth's voice held strain. "God knows whether I'll get there in time," he said. "Drop me at the next turn. I'll make better time cutting across the park."

Nita nodded, cut to the curb. "Good luck, Dick!" she said. It was no more than a whisper. His hand rested on her arm for a moment, his lips brushed the curls that were soft about her temple, then he was striding across the park. Nita watched him go with a piteous quiver of her lips. She knew so fully the altruism that drove Wentworth into this ceaseless service. To an extent, she, too was dedicated. But basically she, like Jackson and Ram Singh, followed a man, and not a cause. It was a hard road, and the rewards were few.

She stilled the quiver of her lips, and lifted her head proudly, though unshed tears glistened on her long lashes. No woman she knew shared her husband's life as fully as she shared Richard Wentworth's. He had no secrets from her, no reticences.

Nita forced a smile to her lips, stilled the worry in her heart and drove quietly to the post to which Wentworth had assigned her. Presently, she might have a chance to serve him again!

WENTWORTH'S JAW was grimly set as he strode into the Capitol. His plans were already made. He could add nothing to the protective measures which would be taken by the Secret Service. But the Master would know about those, and would be prepared to circumvent them. Consequently, there was only one way to protect Senator Marquette and make sure the information he possessed could be used effectively.

Wentworth's hands strayed briefly to the leather girdle he wore beneath his vest. His preparations were made. There were two compactly powerful smoke bombs there, and two of tear gas!

No one prevented him from entering the Senate cloak-room. His presence, his air of assurance had taken him past more formidable barriers. Once inside, he went swiftly to work. Catching up a sheet of notepaper, wrote rapidly:

Senator Marquette:
Your life is in danger the moment you begin to speak. The Master

*intends to kill you. I may be able to offer protection if you will give me
two minutes conversation in the cloakroom before you start. I have
further information about the spies and the Master to amplify your
exposure. Come at once if you wish to survive to make your speech.*

Wentworth's hand went unhesitatingly to his vest pocket and
slipped out his cigarette lighter. Shielding the paper with his
body, he pressed upon it… *the seal of the Spider!*

He realized the risk he ran by that imprint, but there was no
time for halfway measures. The seal would command a respect
that no other signature would achieve. Rapidly, he slid the note
into an envelope, sealed it and beckoned to a page.

"This must be put into Senator Marquette's hands at once,
before he begins his speech," he said quietly. "I cannot exagger-
ate its importance."

The boy nodded alertly and darted from the cloakroom.
The Master of Men was served even by strangers. Wentworth
glanced quickly about him and noted that the room was deserted
except for two men near the entrance to the Senate Chamber.
Everyone had crowded into the chamber to hear Marquette's
speech. Wentworth's blue-gray eyes were darkened with concern.
Unless the Senator heeded the summons, he was certain the
speech would never be made!

There was also an excellent chance that the Senator would
send the Secret Service to seize the Spider!

Wentworth moved close to the door which opened into the
Chamber. He stood against the wall and slid the two smoke
bombs into his palms. His face showed no alarm, but his eyes
were quick and alive. If Senator Marquette came, and would

listen to reason, there would be no difficulty. Even if he proved obdurate, Wentworth thought that he had the means to persuade Marquette to accompany him!

But if the Secret Service came....

Two doors of the cloakroom were suddenly thrown open! Men plunged through them in driving wedges, guns in their fists!

Wentworth did not wait to be spotted by the charging squads of men. The mere opening of the doors was enough to warn him. As one group rushed past him, he dropped a smoke bomb under their feet. The other sailed accurately into the path of the second squad. The simultaneous burst of both was drowned in the rasp of feet, an insignificant sound.

The next instant, billowing black masses of chemical vapor mushroomed from the floor! There was an instant when men cried out in muted surprise before whirling frantically about seeking the author of the attack. And they did not see Wentworth! That was because they did not think to look among their own ranks. Wentworth, gun in hand, was charging forward with the rest, shouting angrily with them, as he joined the hunt for the Spider! Dick Wentworth hunting the Spider?

It lasted only a moment, until the black smoke obscured everything. Men plunged blindly through the vapor, which enveloped all light. In their wild efforts, they lost all sense of direction, fumbled about in confusion.

But Wentworth knew exactly where he was. He stepped back from the mêlée, stole quietly to the door into the Senate Chamber. He opened it a crack. There was no alarm in there.

The soundproofing of the walls and door effectively shut out all sound! At last his opportunity had come!

"Close the doors!" he called into the cloakroom. "Don't let anybody out! The Spider is in here!"

Then he slipped through into the Senate Chamber, let the door click shut. In the next instant, he heard a man's hands strike against the panel, heard a bolt shot home in the lock!

A slight smile moved Wentworth's lips. The Secret Service men had locked themselves in!

BUT THE smile faded quickly, as his eyes swept over the floor of the Senate. Senator Marquette arose and stood beside his desk. The secretary opened his brief case for him, looking up respectfully into the seamed and stern face of the Lion of Wisconigan. Marquette was getting ready to speak!

As he rose to his feet, silence dropped upon the Senate. The talking of the galleries died to a buzz, to a whisper, and faded out....

The walls of the Chamber were lined with standing men. Wentworth knew that there was a plentiful sprinkling of Secret Service operatives among them, of course. And somewhere in this very room, either in the galleries, or perhaps on the floor itself, were the servants of the Master!

There was now small chance of kidnapping Senator Marquette into safety. But the Spider did not hesitate. He moved quietly forward, walking with authority down the central aisle of the Chamber. High on his platform, the Vice President of the United States was slapping his gavel upon the rostrum.

The sergeant-at-arms called for order, and Senator Marquette was on his feet.

Wentworth's eyes were fixed on the Senator, on the white-haired secretary, Stickney, at his side. Stickney was sorting over papers swiftly in the opened briefcase. He turned his head and glanced, almost furtively it seemed to Wentworth, toward the cloakroom door!

An oath lifted to Wentworth's lips as he paced steadily onward. A new suspicion sprang into his mind. He knew suddenly that Marquette had never seen his note; and that it had been the secretary who had sent the police after him when he put through his call to the Senator. What better weapon could the Master employ against Marquette—than the treachery of his private secretary!

It was because this fresh suspicion sharpened his attention that Wentworth watched Stickney pour a glass of water for Senator Marquette. No other eyes than those of the Spider could have spotted the infinitely swift movement of Stickney's hand, which curiously enough was gloved. But Wentworth saw.... He saw Stickney empty a white powder into the Senator's drinking water!

A shout lifted to Wentworth's lips as Marquette accepted the glass. He was still thirty feet away... and the Senator was lifting the glass to his mouth.

"Senator Marquette!" he snapped. *"Don't drink that water! It's poisoned!"*

Heads swung sharply toward Wentworth. He bounded forward. At the same instant, Secret Service men darted from all directions. Senator Marquette either did not hear, or did not understand the cry. The glass was at his lips!

Wentworth's jaws clamped hard together. His right hand moved with a speed the eye could not follow, suddenly was still with an automatic in his fist! In the same split-second, he squeezed the trigger!

The crash of the shot was a thunderclap in the Senate. The instant he fired, Wentworth leaped aside between the rows of the Senators' desks. The legislators were rushing to their feet, and the Secret Service men could not fire.

But Senator Marquette stood like a man turned to ice. He stared vacantly at his hand. It no longer held a glass, for the Spider's bullet had shattered it into a thousand fragments!

But Wentworth did not check his forward race. Stickney was facing him now holding a small, powerful gun! The Spider's disguised face set in a stern mold. If Stickney had to die to preserve the Senator's life, the Spider had no compunction! In his own swift mind, Stickney stood convicted of an attempt to murder Marquette!

As Wentworth lifted his gun slowly, deliberately, he caught a movement just beside him. One of the Senators had run after him, was attacking! He ducked, but it was too late. The Senator swung his water jug and it glanced across the back of Wentworth's skull!

The blow did not knock him out. It sent him reeling, off-balance, as the room whirled before his eyes. He caught himself with an arm braced on a desk. His gun held limply in his other hand.

Deliberately, he let his knees sag, thumped down to the floor. Stickney could not shoot him from that position. His own vision was not clear enough to take a shot at Marquette's secretary without danger of wounding some other innocent. Even to save his own life, the Spider would not do that.

"Senator Marquette!" he called clearly. "Don't make your speech until you have talked to me!"

The next instant, his assailant's hands clamped on his arms. The gun was twisted from his hand, he was yanked to his feet. His vision was clearing a little, he could see Senator Marquette plainly. The man was peering at him, almost vacantly, as he stood beside his desk. For a moment he stared while the Secret Service men hustled Wentworth toward the doors.

Then he swung about heavily. "Mr. President!" his resonant voice lifted. "Let this be the proof of what I am about to say! An attempt has been made upon my life upon the sacred floor of the Senate Chamber!"

He started toward the rostrum with a sheaf of papers in his hand. Stickney was left behind at the desk. The other Senators were taking their seats again and the galleries were quieting.

WENTWORTH TWISTED his head about to stare toward Marquette. Useless to call out to him again. But it was the vacantness of the Senator's stare that worried him. The man had seemed scarcely aware of his surroundings, of what was happening. Yet his cry to the Vice President had been clear and sane enough.

Sane!

Abruptly, Wentworth braced his muscles and wrenched the

two men who held him prisoner. Senator Marquette stood at the microphone on the rostrum now, but the proud power of his carriage was strangely lacking. His leonine head sagged forward, and his arms hung loosely at his sides. The Senate was quiet, waiting....

"Come along," one of the Secret Service men hissed in Wentworth's ear. "Make another disturbance, *and I'll brain you!*"

He wrenched Wentworth's right arm behind him, sending a pain up to his shoulder. He was boosted forward toward the entrance, now no more than ten feet away. Still, he stared back at Senator Marquette.

The Senator's head was lifting, and the shock of what he saw sent a curse to Wentworth's lips. Marquette's powerful face was lax and stupid. His mouth lolled open. A dribble of saliva coursed down over his chin, threaded to his vest front.

A whisper of amazement ran across the floor. One of the clerks stepped to the Senator's side and took hold of his unyielding arm. The senator's head swung around heavily, and without warning the Lion of Wisconigan... *giggled.*

It was a thin, infantile sound. It struck with horror across the Senate Chamber. Somewhere a whisper rose.

"Good Lord!" a man gasped. "Senator Marquette... He's had a stroke! He's... *He's insane!*"

It was at that moment that Wentworth saw Stickney snatch the speech from Marquette's hand!

At the same instant, Wentworth flung himself into action. He called on the superbly powerful muscles of his body to free him of his two captors. He did not attempt to wrench his right arm out of the hammer-lock. Instead he flung himself into a somersault! His left hand twisted free of the grip of the Secret Service man on that side. As his feet struck the floor, he brought the left over in a driving straight-arm that smashed accurately to the point of his captor's jaw. The man's hands ripped away, and Wentworth struck again.

His two captors sprawled to the floor. Other Secret Service men, on guard at the door, sprang toward him. Wentworth flung a tear-gas bomb at their feet, whirled and raced toward Senator Marquette and the ubiquitous Stickney.

The whole Chamber was in turmoil in the same moment. A panic started in the galleries, and the shouts of guards lifted hoarsely. But Wentworth ignored all those things. Two clerks were with Senator Marquette now, trying to move him toward the exit. He was childishly stubborn against their urging hands. His head was tilted back, and he stared toward the galleries as a child might stare at a bright, new toy.

But Stickney was running across the width of the Chamber. He had the speech in one hand, and the small, powerful gun in the other!

Wentworth himself had been disarmed by the Secret Service men, but he did not stop on that account. He snatched up a water jug from a desk and raced on. He knew now that Senator Marquette had gathered terrifically important information, which was incorporated in his speech. Otherwise, the Master would not have troubled to strike at him so terribly. Otherwise, Stickney would not be taking this incredible risk to escape with the text!

The secretary's face twisted about, and it was pale beneath the gray cap of his hair. His eyes held a fierce glitter. Close against the wall, he stopped and whipped up the revolver! In the same moment, Wentworth hurled the water bottle with a perfect aim. The jug caught the outstretched gun-arm, drove it wildly aside, and the weapon clattered from Stickney's hand. His arm dropped limply to his side, and pain distorted his face. He turned and ran, wildly, blindly, toward the corner of the room from which there was no exit!

A triumphant shout lifted to Wentworth's lips. A gun crashed behind him and he heard the vicious whine of a bullet over his head. He did not even face about. He had Stickney now, and there was no thought of personal safety in his mind.

Once let him get hold of that speech, and the Spider would take his chances with the law!

THERE WAS a sudden, shattering blast in the Chamber. Wentworth wavered in his stride, flung a swift glance over his shoulder. Bits of paper flew wildly through the air by Senator Marquette's desk where a blaze had started. And the briefcase in which he had carried his records and evidence had disappeared! No question of what had happened. Stickney had exploded an incendiary bomb in the briefcase—and Stickney himself held the last bit of evidence that Marquette had gathered!

With a harsh oath, Wentworth flung himself forward more swiftly. Stickney was in the far corner of the room. He whirled now, realizing that he was trapped. The speech was still in his free hand. Suddenly, he turned his back on the Senate Chamber, bent his head far forward. His shoulders worked. The devil! He was wedging the speech into his mouth!

Wentworth smiled grimly, knowing he could not destroy it in time. Suddenly Wentworth staggered under a sudden blow on the side of the head. He caught himself, realizing that a thrown gavel had struck him. On the high rostrum, the Vice President stood on his feet, shaking his fists angrily in the air. His lined face was furiously red beneath his white hair. He caught up a water glass and threw it, following it with a book.

Wentworth dodged and leaped on… Stickney was standing up straight now—as straight as any soldier. Something in the man's pose told Wentworth the truth. He was preparing to sacrifice himself to destroy the papers! Wentworth retrieved the book that the vice president had flung, hurled it violently at Stickney's head! The book flew truly. It caught the secretary on the back of the skull, and Stickney's head… *exploded!*

One instant, the man stood there in that braced sacrificial attitude, his head thrown back almost proudly. The next, his headless trunk was sagging to its knees, slumping sideways to the floor. The legs kicked convulsively, as life left him.

Wentworth was still running forward. He flung himself down on his knees beside the horrid corpse that had been the secretary to Senator Marquette. His mind was dazed. Had the book done this? But he knew that was impossible. The man had stuffed the manuscript into his mouth with precisely this in mind. He must have had a fulminate of mercury cap in his pocket. A quick bite with his teeth would have set it off and destroyed the speech!

Wentworth flung the body over on its back. The gloved hands

flung out laxly. Beneath him was a single torn fragment of paper. Wentworth snatched it up… but there was no time to look at it. A quick glance showed him that the Secret Service men had ringed him in. Their line was flung about him in a semi-circle, bottling him in the corner beside the rostrum.

Wentworth lifted a hand of the dead man, and peeled off the glove. An oath leapt to his lips! But he should have expected it! There was small likelihood that Stickney would turn against his employer after a score of years of faithful service. The man on the floor was an impostor. As his hands plainly showed, he was… *Chinese!*

When Wentworth straightened and turned to face the slowly converging cordon of government men, he had a folded paper in his hand. He glanced at them coolly. There was now no chance of recovering the evidence which Senator Marquette had gathered. Stickney, the real Stickney, obviously was dead also. The impostor had ample time to destroy the records in Marquette's office, as he had done away with all that had been brought to the floor of the Senate.

No, nothing else could be done here… but it was now more imperative than ever that the Spider make his escape! He had to find—and destroy—the Master!

His eyes whipped past the cordon of Secret Service men to where Senator Marquette still pettishly fought off those who would lead him from the rostrum. And Marquette's head was tilted back. His eyes were focused… on the gallery!

Wentworth stared where Marquette was looking and a slow fury began to burn its way through his veins. There was one man still seated in the gallery. He was in the first row, directly opposite Marquette. He leaned both arms on the railing and peered down at the Senator. His head was completely bald and deeply cynical lines drawn from his thin-bridged nose down to his mouth comers. But it was his eyes that held Wentworth's attention. Even at this distance, he could feel the force of the man. Those eyes were black, enormous, unblinking. It seemed to Wentworth that red fires burned in their depths!

And in the same moment, Wentworth knew who this man was!

The *Master* had come to make sure that Senator Marquette did not speak! *The Master himself!*

Even as Wentworth spotted the man, he saw the Master push slowly to his feet. The bald head nodded slightly as if in satisfaction at a task well done. The Master turned toward the door!

And the one man who might challenge his powers was unarmed, ringed in by a dozen Secret Service men, helpless under the muzzles of government guns! The Spider!

CHAPTER 6
THE MASTER'S TRAIL

B UT WENTWORTH made no wild dash against those ready guns. The Spider's life was too precious now.

Instead, he bowed to the Secret Service men very formally. He turned toward the rostrum, and lifted the folded paper toward the angry, red-faced man who stood there.

"Mr. President!" Wentworth called, walking toward the rostrum. "Mr. President, I demand the right to be heard!"

"I can point out for you," he called, "the man who murdered Stickney! The man who drove Senator Marquette out of his mind! I can name for you the criminal whom Marquette was going to expose!"

He was no more than two yards from the nearest guns now. The Secret Service men eyed him warily, but waited for an answer from the vice president, who was thumping the desk with his fists. A few of the government agents glanced toward the rostrum. And it was for this moment that Wentworth had gambled.

Without any apparent preliminary tightening of his muscles, he flung himself at the Secret Service men! His hands stabbed out, and two agents were hurled aside as neatly as any all-American tackle ever blocked out opposing linesmen. They spilled against their companions and Wentworth was through the cordon in the same instant, sprinting across the Senate floor!

He cut around a group of milling senators, bounded to the top of a desk and sailed through the air in a perfect aerialist's dive! His leap was perfectly calculated. His outstretched hands hooked the edge of the balcony. The force of his leap swung his legs under it, and he thrust his feet against the ceiling… swung them back, upward, completed a backflip over the railing and into the gallery!

As his hands left the railing, he felt the jar of a bullet sinking into the wood of the gallery door. He felt his coat jerk to the whip of flying lead. Then he popped through the door… and stopped.

The passageway beyond this door, through which the Master had passed only a few seconds before, was empty of all human life!

Wentworth hesitated only an instant. The stairway ahead was the only exit to this corridor… Wentworth raced toward it. The sudden loud shouting that echoed into the rotunda told him that Secret Service men were ahead of him. His lips closed in a grim line. That did not matter! If the chase of the Master led this way, the Spider would brave hell itself to catch him!

His plunging race took him to the gallery around the crowded rotunda. A gray-uniformed guard threw up a gun and blasted at him, but the bullet flew wide. Wentworth sprinted around the gallery, his eyes ever combing the crowds below, seeking a glimpse of the Master. It was in vain. The man had vanished!

Probably, he had slipped into some disguise, but any chance of locating him among that shuffling crowd was lost. He could not even be sure that the man was genuinely bald. It was one of the simplest and cleverest tricks, which he knew from long experience, to assume a characteristic that was extremely conspicuous. The Master need only remove a fake bald covering for his head.

It was maddening to know that the man was so close, practically within reach of the Spider's hand, and yet he was unable to locate him. Another gun-crash echoed through the rotunda, and a chip of marble flew from a column. Wentworth felt the sting of it as it gashed his cheek. Still, he did not flee.

The corridor abruptly echoed to the slap of running feet. The stairs were blocked with armed men who crept upward. Wentworth swore and sprinted down the opposite corridor. He leaped aside into a window niche, thrust an elbow through the glass and sprang to the ledge outside. A moment's hesitation, and he swung down to a column that ran to the portico. His hands burned on the rough stone. The impact of landing numbed his feet. He hit the ground running, heard a woman's clear voice calling to him.

"*This way!*"

WENTWORTH CAUGHT sight of Nita standing boldly on the running board of the rented car. In an instant she ducked inside, whipped the car forward. But he did not run toward the sedan. Instead he flung himself into the street and sprinted. Nita caught his idea instantly, and cut between him and the Capitol. In a split second he took a handhold, eased his feet to the running board.

Nita cut around a corner and Wentworth battled open a door and got into the rear. Somewhere behind, a police siren cut the air with a heart-breaking sound. The radio was on, and a riot of announcements issued from the speaker. Within minutes of Wentworth's escape, radio cars had been sent to block every exit to the city. Someone had spotted the license number of their car.

"There's adhesive tape in my handbag," Nita called quietly. "I heard the whole thing over the radio. They found your note to Marquette. They are accusing the Spider of murdering Stickney, and driving Senator Marquette insane. There was a New York broadcast. Government agents have officially blamed you for Miller's death. They say you have undoubtedly thrown in with an espionage ring." Nita's voice trembled with anger. "Oh, Dick! Why do you keep up this fighting! If only they would not battle against you all the time!"

Wentworth had finished doctoring the splinter gash in his cheek. "The river bank, Nita," he directed quietly.

Nita threw the wheel over and speeded through back streets. Any police car was a hazard, but they dared not proceed on foot. Wentworth was too conspicuous now.

He took a small, powerful automatic from Nita's purse, weighed it on his palm. It was their only weapon. He smiled thinly. Had it been in his possession a short while ago, the Master would no longer be a menace! He could thank the government men for his failure—But how were they to know that he was a savior?

"I managed to salvage one bit of Marquette's speech," he said quietly. "It has three words on it. 'Hoffman Island today.'"

Nita glanced at his reflection in the rear vision mirror. "Hoffman Island?" she said hesitantly. "It's in New York harbor, of course. Down near Staten Island." Wentworth nodded. "It's the Quarantine Hospital of the government," he said. "Persons with contagious diseases are taken off incoming ships and placed there."

Nita frowned, shook her head. "You think the spies' headquarters is there?"

Wentworth jacked open the automatic to make sure there was a cartridge in the chamber. "I think it unlikely," he said. "But I remember reading, a few days ago, that fifty people are quarantined on the island. They are the crew and passengers of a small steamer. Five of them have already died of cholera!"

Nita gasped. "They wouldn't, Dick!" she cried. "The Master wouldn't release cholera germs!" There was no conviction in her voice, only a protest of horror. She knew the Master was fully capable of any crime.

"He wouldn't cause an epidemic," Wentworth said quietly. "But he could plant them, say, in a few selected industrial plants, munitions works, steel plants, or airplane factories. He could cripple our country's industry, by judicious distribution of the plague! But it's only a guess—so far!"

Nita's face was deathly pale. "No, Dick, it's not a guess. I heard a brief bulletin a little while ago. I'd forgotten it in my… my excitement over the senator. Twelve men escaped from Quarantine. Less than an hour ago!"

Wentworth swore harshly. "Nita, I'll drop you at the next corner. Take a taxi to the airport and keep your eyes open!"

"But, Dick!"

Wentworth climbed over the back of the seat. "There's no time to be lost, Nita! The Master is here in Washington, but his

NITA VAN SLOAN

men go on working! We must stop them before they destroy our nation!" Nita slammed on the brakes, opened her door. Wentworth's eyes burned into hers. "If I don't show at the airport within a half hour, get through to Kirkpatrick by telephone and tell him what I believe. Yes, I know it's dangerous to admit I'm in Washington when the Spider has shown here, but it can't be helped!

Nita leaned toward him. There was no smile on her full lips, and her eyes were dark with fear.

"Yes, Dick," she whispered.

For a moment their lips clung, and then Nita stepped back and Wentworth slammed the car away. He crashed a light at the next corner, whirled left on screaming tires and shot out of sight. Nita set her teeth on her nether lip. For an aching moment she waited there, staring the way he had gone. Then she turned blindly down the side street. In the distance, a police siren whimpered on the trail. A squad car roared past, filled with grimly intent riflemen.

NITA'S WHOLE body was rigid with the necessity of maintaining a normal appearance. She turned her head to watch the heavy machine thunder past and her eyes strained wide with fear. Her heart thudded with sickening force. Those rifles were meant for... Dick!

She turned away with a smothered sob, and found a taxi at the next corner.

"To the airport," she ordered, and her soft voice had a harsh undertone.

She knew what Dick planned to do at the airport, and she knew the danger into which he would walk... danger from which he had thrust her aside! He planned to steal a plane, as the only way to break the police barrier around the capital. And the police would be expecting some such move.

"Hurry!" she snapped at the sleepy taxi driver, thinking of the cruel rifles.

Nita forced herself to relax as Wentworth had taught her. The drive to the airport seemed endless. She paid off her driver, walked steadily into the administration building. To avert suspicion, she booked a passage on the next New York plane. But when she gave her name, the uniformed attendant looked up with a quick smile.

"There is a chartered plane at your disposal, Miss van Sloan," he said. "Your pilot arrived ten minutes ago, and the plane is warming up."

Nita managed an acknowledging smile, then, in bewilderment, followed the attendant. A long-nosed Lockheed was blasting on the line. As she neared it, the helmeted pilot cut the motor and sprang down from the cockpit. Nita caught her breath. The face she did not know, but there could be no mistaking the pilot's lithe efficiency of movement. It was Dick!

Not until they had taken off under the very eyes of the patrolling police did Nita speak over the intercommunicating phone. She heard Wentworth laugh softly.

"I played in luck," he said.

Nita leaned back in the seat and closed her eyes. Easy for Dick, yes. The escape had been simplified, but there would be pursuit. All Washington was armed against the Spider; in New York, they were hunting for Richard Wentworth. But Dick was intent only on his own quest....

Wentworth spoke presently, his tone crisp. "I've learned by radio that the police have caught nine of the twelve cholera cases on Staten Island. The other three have disappeared completely. They are munitions workers."

"There are munitions works in both Jersey and Delaware," Nita said, thoughtfully.

"I think there is no doubt," Wentworth's tone was savage, "that the Master maneuvered the whole thing and that he has helped those men to disappear. Undoubtedly, he is transporting them to those munitions plants. He will already have arranged for them to get jobs, possibly by fixing up a substitution scheme.

Unless we can stop him, he will cripple those plants by spreading wholesale death! Forcing a quarantine. And once the cholera gets loose, it may be impossible to check it."

Nita twisted her narrow white hands together and did not answer. She turned her head slowly to stare back into Dick's goggled eyes. The wind loosened the hair under her helmet, whipped its tendrils like small flails against her cheeks. She gathered strength and courage from him.

"Outerbridge Crossing?" she asked.

Wentworth nodded. "That's the most direct route to the munitions plants."

"But how will they transport those men without danger of becoming infected themselves?" Nita asked. "Certainly not by a passenger car?"

"Possibly in a closed truck, with a separate cab," Wentworth suggested.

Nita faced forward again, crouching in the shelter of the windshield. How in the world would Dick spot the right transport? She could not guess, but she never doubted his ability. Too many times, he had snatched victory from defeat; performed the impossible. She stole one more glance at him.

Wentworth's eyes stabbed fiercely ahead to the horizon. His kindly mouth, disguised now, was set in an inflexible line. So far, the radio told him, their trick had not been discovered, but the chase could not be long delayed. He did not fear pursuit by anything less than the army and navy ships, but they would certainly be employed. Not only was his own plane unarmed, but he could not fight against the men who served his country. Neither would he turned aside from his quest.

THE PLANE was still ten minutes from Outerbridge when the inevitable radio message came rasping over the air. But Wentworth held to his course and presently swung in a wide circle over the long bridge that connected Staten Island with New Jersey. Traffic was virtually at a standstill on the island highway, backed up for a mile or more. Police were busy at the bridgehead.

"Perhaps the police will find them!" Nita's voice phrased his own thought.

Wentworth shook his head. "The Master will have anticipated that search," he said.

His eyes quested over the traffic, but what could he hope to distinguish from this height? The escaping men might be in any one of those vehicles. In fact, as nearly as Wentworth could figure it, the time lapse was about right.

Nita's voice came through sharply, saying, "Three planes taking off from Governors' Island!"

Wentworth lifted his eyes to the harbor of New York, to the towers of the skyscrapers shrouded in the haze. The three planes from the island fortress were climbing at high speed. There was only one recourse: He must abandon the stolen Lockheed at once! He had laid his plans, having spotted a possible landing field near an isolated filling station a few miles away in New Jersey. But he must lose no time!

He whipped the Lockheed about in a steep *reversement* and in a minute's time side-slipped with frantic speed toward the earth. Nita had the glasses to her eyes, peering back toward the flight of army planes.

"I think we're spotted." Her voice was calm. "They swung about and headed this way."

Wentworth nodded, but made no other reply. His gaze was focused on the field that rushed up toward them. A man ran out from under the filling station shed, his face upturned. The car Wentworth had noticed was still parked beside it.

Nita's voice faltered, "They're incredibly fast," she said.

A scant hundred feet above the earth, Wentworth ruddered out of the sideslip, slashed toward a landing. He fish-tailed to kill his speed, set the Lockheed down gently.

"I'll go first," he told Nita. "As soon as I begin talking to that man, jump out and follow."

"Yes," she acknowledged. "The planes will be overhead in about two minutes." So perfectly had Wentworth calculated the speed and roll of his ship that it came to a halt within twenty feet of the filling station. Wentworth cut the motor, leaped to the wing in the same moment and bounded to the ground. He ran toward the garage man.

"Police business!" he called. "Have you got a phone?"

The man nodded, turned, about to point… and Wentworth was upon him. A swift compression of nerve centers in the man's throat, and he sagged unconscious to the earth. As Wentworth carried him toward the filling station, Nita was racing beside him. He tossed her the keys he had fumbled from the unconscious man's pocket.

"Get the car started," he cried. "Check the gas!"

Nita darted to follow his orders, heard Wentworth's sharp footfalls as he ran toward a second car in the garage. She heard the hood clatter up as she jumped behind the wheel. She was driving the stolen sedan swiftly up the concrete, Wentworth tense beside her when, a moment later, they heard the mounting whine of a power-diving plane.

"Why are we going away from Outerbridge?" she asked, and her voice was a gasp.

"Have to lose this car, get another," Wentworth told her crisply. "Cut left at that crossroads. Skid into it."

Nita's driving was second only to Wentworth's. She hit the turn with the gas pedal jammed to the floor, in a screaming of tires. Even above that racket, she heard the heavy chatter of a machine gun, the thunder of the diving plane. She had a glimpse of bullet-powdered concrete leaping up in the path they had been following only a moment before.

She leaned far forward over the wheel, and fought the bucking wheel. The road plunged into the shade of over-arching trees. A village street opened ahead of her, and at Wentworth's quiet command, she eased on the throttle. The roaring fury of the planes was overhead, but they couldn't use their guns here. Other cars were in the street ahead. Nita eased in among them, realizing then that her hands were trembling on the wheel. People were running into the street, staring upward.

"The third plane landed back there by the gas station," Wentworth said quietly. "We leave this car here. Turn right. Trees there. Circle back at the next corner and park. I'll meet you there."

At Nita turned under the trees Wentworth dropped out to the street. She realized he had shed his flying jacket and helmet. They lay on the floor beside her. She ripped off her own borrowed helmet, followed Wentworth's orders.

She parked the car and strolled toward the corner of the main street. The planes still circled and swooped overhead. She gaped at them, as everyone else was doing.

MOMENTS LATER, she saw Wentworth driving a car with a battered fender. He was without hat or coat, and there was a wide smile on his face as he poked open the door.

"Hi, there, Gladys!" he called. "Can I give you a lift?"

Nita tossed her curls. "Depends on where you're going," she said.

"Just out riding, but it's a swell day!"

Nita laughed and climbed in. "Don't care if I do, Sam," she said.

If anyone heard their actual words, at least no one paid any attention. Wentworth still seemed to be laughing at their joke as he explained. "Bought it from a boy for twice what it's worth. He thinks I'm a G-man, escaping from crooks. He'll be safe, I told him, if he stays in the movie for four hours. If there are G-men in those planes it won't work, but I think they're just army pilots without detective training."

The car trundled along at a moderate speed and soon they were on the Outerbridge Road. The army planes still circled over the village.

Wentworth's eyes flicked keenly over the widely spaced traffic that filtered through from Staten Island. All the cars were traveling fast, trying to make up for the time lost by the police search. Nita kept up an animated pretense of talk in case keen eyes should be watching them.

"Now what?" she asked presently.

Wentworth answered without taking his eyes off the traffic. "There's a tourist camp near the bridge, this side. We'll park there for an hour. If we haven't spotted our quarry in that time, we'll get in touch with the munitions works, take up our watch there. We'll have to separate in that case."

They spent a long and mostly silent hour at the tourist camp. Trucks and passenger cars rolled past at long intervals from the bridge. Wentworth watched each one with a narrow concentration, searching for any incongruity. Once they leaped into the car and followed a milk tanker for a few miles until Wentworth could catch a closer view of the driver's face. A dynamite truck aroused Nita's suspicions temporarily. But the hour passed without a definite discovery and Wentworth was turning away from the search to try the second plan he had outlined when his attention centered on a steel truck just cresting the rise above them.

"Wait!" he said sharply. "I never heard of a steel fabrication plant on Staten Island!"

He caught up the glasses that Nita had brought from the plane, focused them keenly. "Nothing unusual about the driver," he said. "The cab is isolated, but the trailer is open. Nowhere for anyone to hide except under the beams."

Nita said swiftly, "A truck like that wouldn't be searched very closely, would it?"

The truck was now gathering speed down the slope.

"Those steel beams are stacked pretty high!" Wentworth said quietly. "I should say the truck was over the load limit… if they're solid steel! By the heavens, Nita, that truck belongs to France Steel!"

Without a further word, Nita started the engine of their car. She cut the wheels in a sharp turn, rolled to the edge of the road to wait until the truck rolled past. Wentworth kept the glasses on the driver. This was pre-arranged. Wentworth wanted to alarm the driver if he were guilty; wanted him to know he had fallen under suspicion.

The driver glanced at them sharply as the truck rolled past. He was alone in the cab. Nita immediately sent the noisy sedan spurting out into the roadway, and took the trail no more than a hundred feet behind the truck.

"Is this it?" she asked softly.

Wentworth was frowning. "Can't be sure," he answered. "I'd swear there were no false beams in that load. They're all steel. But there might be a pocket under them. Follow for a while, but hold this distance."

The truck was laboring up another rise, but Nita kept the old car squarely behind it. She speeded up when the truck spurted down the slope beyond.

"He's doing better than sixty," she said, observing the speed-ometer.

Wentworth nodded, continued to study the load of steel. At the next crossroads, the truck swung sharply to the left on a much poorer road. When Nita turned into its wake, Wentworth uttered an exultant laugh.

"We've got it, Nita!" he cried. "The driver has pulled a gun! There's a long hill on the other side of that bridge below. We'll take him there!"

HALF WAY up the next slope, the truck rushed on the momentum of its downward swoop; then its speed dwindled. At Wentworth's instructions Nita ran the car close against the protruding beams at the rear of the steel truck. Wentworth clambered out on the running board, forward over the hood, and jumped to the trailer. Instantly, he was leaping forward over the load of steel beams. His gun glinted in his fist.

"Stop the truck!" he commanded. "It's the police!"

He saw the driver's angry face glaring back at him through the rear window of the cab. Noticing the man's hesitation he leveled the automatic.

"Stop the truck!" he repeated coldly. "You haven't got a chance!"

He heard Nita gun the old car up beside the long trailer, but his attention held implacably on the driver, who was at a total disadvantage. Before he could twist around to bring his gun to bear, Wentworth could blast out his life!

Wentworth saw a look of resolution harden the driver's face, but before he had a chance to fire, the man hurled himself sideways to the seat! Suddenly there was a violent wrench in the movement of the trailer! Wentworth heard beneath him the squeal of steel slipping on steel, the shift of the massive beams!

A wild cry lifted in his throat. A man of slower perception would have been trapped, crushed to death among those steel beams. Wentworth's superb co-ordination sent him sideways

113

in a frantic leap. There was no time to choose a landing place. A split-second after the first wrench of the trailer, Wentworth was in the air, sprawling toward the earth.

Even as he flew wildly through space, Wentworth realized the thing that had happened with the speed of flying bullets. By that sideways jump the driver had uncoupled the trailer from the tractor by some special mechanism which the Master had arranged in advance! The powerful engine of the tractor, ripped wide open, and the drag of the overloaded trailer accomplished the rest. In a flash, the two parts of the truck pulled apart!

As the tractor, freed of its load, shot forward, Wentworth saw a fearful thing. There was a chain secured to the tractor. Its other end vanished into the front end of the load of beams. As Wentworth struck the earth, sprawling on a steep embankment, that chain snapped taut.

He shouted fiercely. Pitching backward with the violence of his fall, he flung a bullet at the cab. It was vain. The chain accomplished its purpose and confirmed Wentworth's guess that there was a secret pocket beneath the load. The chain yanked out a plug of false beams which concealed the pocket, which held up the tons of steel above the place where the three disease-bearing workers were hidden! And the beams collapsed in a roaring clash of heavy steel!

Above the roar of the subsiding beams, the squeal of metal on tortured metal, there lifted a multiple human cry! It was dreadful in its intensity, hoarse with the fear of overwhelming death! For that single moment, while the steel collapsed into the hollow pocket, the cry sounded. It pinched off horribly, crushed out of existence beneath tons of steel!

The Master had laid his plans well! Preparing to spirit away the three men, he had arranged for their elimination in case his plans were penetrated. There would be no testimony now from the three disease carriers!

Fury hurled Wentworth to his feet while that frantic, despairing cry still sounded. His gun was clutched in his hand but, from his position low down on the embankment, he could see only the extreme top of the fleeing cab. It raced up the hill with accelerating speed.

He hurled himself wildly at the grade. Loose dirt and stones avalanched about his spurning feet. He heard the crash of gunfire above, but whether it was Nita or the driver he could not see. Curses panted from his lips. The trailer with its fearful load already had coasted to a halt. As Wentworth fought his way to the brink of the embankment it began to trundle backward down the grade!

At the crest of the hill, the tractor popped out of sight. But Nita....

The trailer was gaining speed. As it ground backward, it cleared the ancient sedan and revealed a white-faced Nita behind the wheel. She did not need his swift gesture. The sedan was already curving toward him. He sprang to the running board.

"I got a tire!" Nita gasped at him. "Oh, that fiend! Those poor men!"

WENTWORTH MADE no attempt to climb into the

car, but clung with one hand, his automatic lifted and ready. If Nita had punctured a tire of the tractor, they stood a chance of overtaking the driver in this wreck of a car. He twisted his head about. Nothing could be done about the trailer. Nothing need ever be done about it now. It was gathering speed wildly as it thundered backward down the grade, carrying its piteous load. The steel beams leaped and sang against one another under the jarring of the mad run. As if they exulted; as if they danced above the humanity they had destroyed.

A spurt of red flame gushed up from between the walloping steel. No, the Master had missed no tricks. He had set a fire, too, to wipe out the last traces of his crime. As Wentworth watched, a rear wheel of the trailer jarred off the concrete of the road, and for a while the whole huge mass continued to parallel the highway. Then it slipped farther down the embankment, and in an instant, the trailer swung about. Its rear dipped while the front sprang joyously into the air. The entire massive trailer leaped clear of the earth in a titan's somersault. Beams scattered from the load like straws in a gust of wind. They whirled, spun, somersaulted in gargantuan play. One struck a pine tree with a three-foot trunk, slicing it through in one clean stroke.

The laboring sedan crested the rise, swooped over the ridge, and the scene was blotted out from Nita and Wentworth. Only the sound was left: the cannonade of giants. It dwindled out of Wentworth's consciousness as his eyes focused on the road ahead.

The tractor had a lead of a full mile. He could see it ahead, weaving all over the road. It jounced wildly under the surge of the tire Nita had punctured. Wentworth saw it slam against the side of a rock cut, carom almost across the road, and then whip out of sight again.

Wentworth was forced to cling to the side of the car with both hands as Nita hurled the sedan into the downgrade. The speed of the flying vehicle stuffed the breath back into his nostrils. His knees gave as they hit the next rise, but he clung on grimly, and waited his chance.

When they bellowed through the rock cut, the distance to their quarry was halved. Wentworth could see the punctured tire flapping loosely on its rim. As he watched, it flung loose and the tractor wrenched wildly. Wentworth could see the frantic bobbing of the driver's head as he fought the heavy wheel. Then the tractor swung broadside, flopped over, its wheels pawing the air. The spin continued, and the tractor smashed, right-side up, against the side of a dirt cut.

FOR A space of seconds, while the sedan thundered nearer and nearer, nothing stirred in the wrecked and battered truck cab. Then the door popped open, and the driver spilled to the ground. He picked himself up and started to run. Realizing his error he reeled toward the road, and whirled around drunkenly to flee the other way before plunging back into the cab of the truck.

As the sedan skittered to a halt a hundred feet from the wreck, Wentworth released his hold. There was a smooth run of sun-burned grass beside the road. Wentworth leaped toward it with a trick he had learned from observation at the G-man school. He somersaulted in the air, checked his speed by that trick, and landed running. He flung himself to the grass as the driver thrust a gun out of the cab's rear window.

The bullet tore up a yard beyond Wentworth. He lifted his small, powerful automatic with deliberation, squeezed off a shot. There was a hoarse cry of pain from the truck. Wentworth fired once more, and metal rang under the punch of the bullet. After a moment, a thin crystal jet of gasoline spilled to the ground beneath the cab.

But Wentworth had not waited for the sure results of that shot. He struck a match and touched it to the sun-dried grass ahead of him. The flames caught, lifted with a thin crackling and began to creep along the ground. The smoke lifted in small blue spirals, began to drift toward the cab.

Wentworth raised his voice coldly. "In about three minutes, or less, your truck will blow up," he said. "I've punctured your gas tank. You can smell the smoke. Come out with both hands over your head, high!"

The man's face showed for a frightened instant at the cab window. He yelled a curse, and his gun blasted wildly through the opening. Wentworth flung a quick glance toward Nita. She was crouched behind the sedan, waiting as he had directed. The shots continued to blast from the window, but they were wild.

"You have about one minute left!" Wentworth called. "The flames are pretty close to the gasoline!"

Silence then for a space of heartbeats, silence in which he could feel the fear of the trapped man. Then there was a single shot. It was not fired through the window, and its sound was muffled.

Wentworth swore, leaped to his feet to run forward. Once before, the Master had cheated him by the suicide of his quarry! Caution checked him ten feet away from the truck. It might be a trick! He balanced his automatic, threw a glance toward the creeping fire. And in that instant, he heard Nita cry out sharply in warning.

He flung himself wildly aside, heard a double blast of gunfire. One was so close that he could smell the acrid sting of burning gunpowder. The other remote shot was Nita's! Wentworth rolled, with his automatic ready, and choked down a bitter oath. The driver was slumping out of the cab to the ground. His body was lax in death, and the side of his head had disappeared.

Nita's heels were crisp and frightened on the concrete. "Dick!" she cried. "Oh, Dick…."

Wentworth pushed slowly to his feet. "I'm still alive, dear," he called quietly. "Thanks to you!"

He reached the dead driver in a stride, flung a swift glance about the interior of the cab.

"That fire!" Nita gasped. "Oh, I'm sorry, Dick! But I could only see the side of his head. He… His gun was pointed right at you!"

Wentworth caught the driver's lax body up from the ground and ran with it toward the sedan. There was a faint smile on his lips as he looked into Nita's white face.

"You have nothing with which to reproach yourself, Nita," he said quietly. "It would have been better to take him alive. But for my carelessness it wouldn't have happened. We'll have to get away from here fast!"

He threw the body into the back of the car, climbed in after it and once again Nita sent the noisy sedan racing forward. Wentworth caught a flash of flame from the corner of his eye as they sped past the wrecked truck cab. The fire had reached the gasoline. As they plummeted down into the valley beyond, there was a rushing roar of an explosion behind them. The white road caught a crimson wash of light for an instant, and then it was gone.

Wentworth was bending over the body of the truck driver, searching it swiftly.

"That will bring people here pretty quickly," he called to Nita, "but we'll have to chance it. Pull off the road by those woods."

She stopped the car and bent her face into her hands. Tremors shook her shoulders. Wentworth was peering down at the things he had extracted from the dead man's pockets. It was a disappointingly small bag. Apparently the man had been a regular driver for France Steel. His driver's license was in order. There was money, a bill of lading for the U.S. Munitions Co., Inc., and a Chinese laundry slip.

Wentworth stared at the slip and shook his head angrily. It was from a shop in the same town in upper Dutchess County in which the France Steel plant was situated. Abruptly, Wentworth stooped over and wrenched open the collar of the man's shirt. He stared at the laundry mark on the collar, and a slow smile came to his lips.

"He carries a Chinese laundry slip," Wentworth said slowly, "but he has his shirts done in another shop. Chinese use an ideograph to identify the shirts. This man's is marked RB-1743."

Nita twisted about to stare at him. "What does it, mean?" she asked shakily.

Wentworth stooped over the dead man, his cigarette lighter poised. He pressed its base against the paling flesh of the forehead.

"It means, my dear," he said happily, "that as soon as I have hidden this minion of the Master securely in the woods, we are going to pay a call on the Master! Unless all my deductive powers fail me, this Chinese laundry slip is the key that will unlock all his mysteries!"

He lifted the cigarette lighter, and on the dead man's forehead there gleamed the bloody blotch of the Spider's seal!

CHAPTER 7
THE CHINESE KEY

NEW FRANCE, where the steel mills were situated, was a model industrial town dropped into the midst of the countryside. The workers lived in neat homes, each with its plot of ground, and there were extensive recreation centers. Buses sped the men to the plant, placed to the leeward of the town. Even the Chinese laundry was set in an incongruously colonial looking block of stores.

The laundry alone showed a light.

The coupé that Wentworth drove was a shabby looking affair, and no one would ever suspect what a powerful motor was hidden under the battered hood. Wentworth drove slowly past the laundry. "It's just a Chinese laundry," Nita said dubiously.

"Sam Lee… He must have forty thousand relatives in this country."

Wentworth made no answer, but drove around the corner to park the coupé. He had altered his disguise again. He retained the predatory nose of the Spider, the lipless gash of a mouth. It would require only the addition of cape and wig to convert him into that dread nemesis. He now took these articles from a secret compartment, folded a special silken cape to pocket size and stowed them away on his person.

"We'll stroll past," he said quietly. "If we find a lookout post, fine. If not, we'll arrange something else."

They found a lookout post a half a block away in a narrow strip of park where there was a bench. They sat close together in the kindly dusk, and Nita dropped her head on his shoulder. But theirs was not lovers' talk, for all their whispering.

They had to wait only a few minutes before the first man stepped up to the door of the laundry, paused a moment before entering.

"Good heavens, what a coat and scarf!" Nita whispered. "There must have been seven colors in each one, and no two of them even blending."

"One of the oldest tricks of disguise," Wentworth told her quietly. "Concentrate everyone's attention on one thing, a bright handkerchief, or an obvious feature—like the Spider's cape and hunchback. They rarely look beyond that."

Presently, the door opened again, and the same vivid coat and scarf were again evident. There was a bundle of laundry beneath the man's arm. Nita relaxed a little.

"He came out again right away," she said. "Maybe we're wrong, Dick!"

Wentworth's arm was taut about her shoulders. "No, my dear, we're right!" he said. "The man who went in wore tan shoes, but this man's shoes are black!" He drew Nita to her feet. "The thing is obvious when you look for it. This is a small town, where ultimately it would be noticed if many men went into that laundry and few came out! So a man, conspicuously dressed, goes inside… behind those steamed up windows! He gives the bright coat and scarf to another man who comes out with a package of laundry. And number one goes on into the Master's hideout!"

Nita said, humbly, "I can see that you're right, Dick. This man doesn't have the same walk. And women are supposed to be observant!"

Wentworth pressed her arm, and they turned the corner in a stroll that nevertheless almost kept pace with the man in the bright coat. "If I'm right," Dick said softly, "he'll enter some house in the same block with the laundry. He must get back there to wear the clothes of the next arrival!"

A few moments later, Wentworth's deduction was confirmed when the man entered a two-story apartment house, almost directly behind the laundry. It was while they were strolling past the entrance that another man came out. He carried a bundle of laundry tied up in a shirt. He was whistling a gay tune and he wore an orange and blue sweater. He entered the laundry and in a normal length of time a man in an orange and blue sweater, whistling the same tune, made his exit without the bundle of laundry.

Nita's hand tightened on Wentworth's arm. "You're right!" she whispered. "Oh, it's so *simple*. And no one would even suspect it!"

But Wentworth guided her toward the coupé. "You'll take your post here. Remain for one hour," he instructed swiftly. "If I'm not out in that time, summon the State Police!"

"But, Dick!"

"I'm not protecting you," Wentworth said quietly. "I'm protecting myself! I don't know what I'm walking into, but there is no other way. For an hour, dear... or less!"

WENTWORTH KISSED her quickly and strolled away. He did not go to the laundry, but to the house on the opposite side of the block. He was in time to follow the man in the orange and blue sweater to an apartment on the ground floor, to see him enter without knocking. Wentworth did the same.

The man he had followed was hanging the orange and blue sweater on a numbered peg. He hurried out of another door without speaking. There were two other men in the room, and their eyes rested on Wentworth sullenly.

"You'll wait your turn," one of them growled.

Wentworth nodded without words, and flung himself into a chair where he busied himself with a cigarette. His eyes rested on the match he struck. Apparently these two men had accepted him without question. That meant that all members of the Master's gang did not know each other. That was excellent! Wentworth lounged back in the chair, but the hand that held the cigarette was always close to the butt of one of his under-arm automatics.

He did not attempt to lay plans. That would be impossi-

124

ble until he had found what lay before him. He had only one object—to find and slay the Master! Nothing less than that would put an end to this stealthy undermining of the country's industries! Meanwhile, Wentworth relaxed, and waited.

When presently, the other two men had made their way out of the apartment, and the substitute returned, Wentworth got quietly to his feet.

The substitute whined at him. "God almighty!" he said. "I've been on the merry-go-round all night. Must be a hell of a big meeting! Not a single mug has come out to ride the merry-go-round for me.

Wentworth grunted, "Ain't that hell!"

The man scowled at him and ducked out the other entrance. As Wentworth hung up his own coat and hat, took down a conspicuous sports jacket of green suede from the wall, two other men came in. Wentworth did not look toward them. On the wall beneath the jacket was a small sign:

"Limp heavily. Right leg."

Wentworth put on the jacket and limped around the block. In his pocket was the ticket, taken from the dead truck driver. His blue-gray eyes, hooded under heavy false brows, were ice cold. His guns were loose in their holsters.

Wentworth walked into the shop, scowled at the Chinese behind the counter and tossed the ticket on the counter. The Chinese shot him a single inimical glance, slapped a slug shaped like a coin down on the wood. Wentworth picked it up. There was a doorway between the laundry racks, covered by a green curtain. Wentworth pushed through it, and peeled off the jacket. The man he had seen in the other apartment came forward.

"Cheez!" he grumbled. "The merry-go-round! It wears me out!"

"Limp pretty," Wentworth jeered at him.

The man glanced at him as he put on the green suede jacket. He caught up a package of laundry and went limping out of the rear room. Wentworth flung a quick look about him. There was the full laundry lay-out, a back door opening into the court behind the shop, and nothing else to indicate an exit! But the Chinese had given him a slug like a coin—and against the wall was a pinball game!

WENTWORTH CROSSED to it quickly, stared down at the arrangement of numbered pockets and baffles into which the balls were to be shot. He frowned, dropped his coin in the slot, and snapped a ball. As the ball sped upward, the main baffle moved aside and the ball shot behind it. There was a click, a whir of machinery—and the floor began to drop deliberately beneath his feet!

It moved steadily, a miniature elevator. A concrete-lined wall was close about him, and it seemed that the drop continued for a long way, fully two stories. But it moved swiftly, until it was flush with a small door. Wentworth opened it hurriedly, stepped through as the elevator halted. As he cleared the lift, it snapped upward with prodigious speed, clicked back into position in the room behind the laundry!

As Nita had said, the thing was simple—beautifully simple!

Undoubtedly, if a nickel were dropped into the slot of the

pinball game, it would operate like any other board. Only a slug of a special weight would make the necessary contact to set the elevator in motion. But there was no time to speculate on the perfection of the Master's arrangements. Wentworth hurried along, narrow, well-lighted corridor of concrete opened ahead of him. Presently, the corridor widened into a chamber, with benches along two sides of the wall. A dozen men filled the seats. Beyond them the corridor ended in a blank wall of concrete.

Wentworth apparently paid no attention at all to these features. He dropped into a vacant place on one of the benches and waited. Occasionally, one of the men spoke to his neighbor in a low growl. Some of the men smoked impatiently. Time dragged on... and nothing happened.

Wentworth schooled himself to relaxation. Surely, within an hour, there would be some development. So many men would not be assembled merely to sit in an underground chamber and grumble. Some secret door would open and then... the Spider would confront the Master!

Four more men made their way singly, at regular intervals, along the corridor and slumped into seats; and another half hour dragged past. Wentworth felt the slow tightening of his nerves. He should have allowed himself more time. It would be disastrous if the police, summoned by Nita according to his orders, crashed in here and caught no more than this group of gangsters. And the work of the Master would go on unmolested!

Wentworth's acutely attuned senses suddenly caught a new sound in this corridor. More than one person was coming. His head swung toward the passageway, and he saw that the others

There was a terrific roar of an explosion behind them.

had noticed the change. One of the men drew out a revolver with a nervous oath. Another jumped to his feet. All eyes burned into the dimness of the corridor that stretched out interminably toward the elevator.

Finally, the two who approached them passed beneath a light. They were Chinese. Their shoulders were bowed, as they dragged something between them.

A sharp fear went through Wentworth as he watched. He could see nothing clearly. The Chinese had moved past the light into shadow. There was only the silhouette of their bowed shoulders, their bobbing heads. Their bodies completely filled the narrow corridor.

Wentworth fought savagely against the fear that dried his throat. It was nonsense to think that… Nita had been captured! Yet that definitely was what he feared. There was no logic in it. He had come through without difficulty. They would have no reason to suspect her. None at all.…

But it required all the will power at his command for Wentworth to turn stolidly back to the bench and flop into the seat. The other men were seating themselves also. He heard one laugh.

"Some fool tried to get in," he said. "Naw! How the hell would I know who?"

The man next to Wentworth grunted with pleasure. "Maybe we'll have some fun then," he said. "Cripes, you need something after this waiting."

Wentworth did not speak, and his hands pulled toward his guns. If it were Nita, he… could do nothing! Not that he doubted his ability to fight this score of men. But... the Master must die! He shifted a little in his seat. This was nonsense, of course. It couldn't be Nita!

EACH SHUFFLING footstep of the two Chinese seemed to fall inside his brain. He schooled himself to show no more curiosity than the others. His eyes burned hotly in their sockets as they probed the advancing shadow of the Chinese. He could see their bowed heads and stooped shoulders. Their hands were behind them, dragging....

A fierce cry drove into Wentworth's throat, and he choked it back. He sat as if carven from rock upon the bench.

Beside him, a man laughed, "I said we'd have fun! Cripes, a dame—hey!"

"Swell looking legs she's got there. Hey, yellow boy, stand her on her head!"

"Trust these chinks to handle a dame. That's the way to treat 'em all right. Me, I always drag my dames by their legs. Knocks sense into their heads."

Wentworth turned his head toward the man beside him. His neck was stiff. "If anything can knock sense into a dame's head," Wentworth said, and laughed.

The sound of his laughter shocked him. He'd better not try that again. He had to force himself to look at the captive woman, being dragged by her ankles along the corridor, to look at... *Nita!* She was conscious. She held her head away from the floor. Her face was deadly pale, and her eyes were almost closed. If she saw Wentworth, she gave no sign at all. For she, too, understood that her capture could make no difference. At all costs, the

Master must be destroyed. If it cost her life, if it cost the Spider's life, the Master must be destroyed!

At the dead end of the corridor, the two Chinese stopped. One of them looked around slowly, but not at Nita. His eyes took in the benches. Every seat was filled. He seemed to do nothing at all, but suddenly there was the muted whir of well-oiled machinery. The end of the corridor receded a full two feet, then rolled smoothly to one side. The Chinese walked on, slowly, dragging Nita. Where she had lain for a moment was a small blur of red on the concrete floor.

The men trooped through noisily, jeering at her. "These chinks know how to handle dames," one of them said again. "I said we'd have fun! Cripes! She's got a shape, too."

Wentworth was not the first nor the last through the doorway, but his keen ears heard the machinery whir again and move that solid chunk of concrete back to plug the entrance. His legs moved automatically, and with the same machinelike precision, he took in the chamber into which they moved. He tried to cut out of his heart and mind the fact that Nita was here, was being tortured. He concentrated on one thought. The Master must die!

There was a white-hot point of fury in the back of his brain. He tried to ignore its presence and held it rigidly in check. If it burst, there would be slaughter. But the Master first!

This first chamber through which they filed was intolerably hot. Up near the ceiling, there were banks of pipes. Faintly, he thought he could detect the jar of machinery operating overhead. His eyes narrowed. It could mean but one thing, and it jibed with the course of the underground passage. This headquarters of the Master was beneath the industrial plant of France Steel! He recognized that fact in a heavy, lethargic way; with a part of his mind that operated without volition on his part. His heart was there with Nita....

Another segment of concrete wall receded and slid aside, and the intense heat of the antechamber was left behind. They stood in a chamber that was the duplicate of the one beneath Chinatown, drapes of golden silk and a deep golden rug underfoot. But there was this difference: instead of a throne chair, there was an altar presided over by a fat-bellied Chinese god. Still the Master was not in sight.

The two Chinese moved directly toward the altar and Wentworth knew a thankfulness at least for the soft carpet which would be easier on Nita's poor back. His fists knotted achingly, and he cut the thought from his mind. But that point of fury within his skull had grown larger.

The time had come when he could plan. The Master must presently enter this place. The battlefield was set... and the enemy forces were all about him. With an effort he pulled his eyes away from Nita, and that threatening altar. His mind was dull, and slow, because of the consuming anger. But he had to think. Even to save Nita, he must think desperately. From this trap, the Spider must snatch a precious life—and victory.

He glanced secretly at the men about him. Like himself, they were in shirt sleeves. Only two others besides Wentworth had retained their vests. All carried guns, either in holster or pocket. FROM THE direction of the altar, there was the thin shriek of torn silk and Nita's shamed and angry cry. The man beside Wentworth laughed exultantly.

"Quiet," Wentworth told himself. *"Quiet, damn you!"*

There was small room in his brain now for anything save that mounting fury. He fumbled into his pockets making his preparations close to his body, rolling the base of his cigarette lighter against the lens of his flashlight.

When that was prepared, he touched the arm of the man beside him. He steeled himself against the anger which the man's lewd face aroused. The man's head swung about impatiently—and his eyes met those of Richard Wentworth, the Master of Men!

Wentworth's blue-gray eyes were wide, and the pinpoint flame of his will burned in their depths. The man's head turned toward him, and his own gaze widened to the shock of that stare. In an instant, expression was blanked from his face. Wentworth reached out to drop an arm carelessly across his shoulders, pressing his fingers firmly into the nape beneath the edge of the skull. By that grip, Wentworth drew the man close—whispered to him fixing him with his glance.

"You are the Spider!" Wentworth whispered.

The man's lips moved stiffly. "I... I am the Spider!" he was whispering, too.

Wentworth felt satisfaction pour warmly through him. He thought he had chosen his subject well, but he had obtained an unusually prompt hypnosis. Probably his subject had been subjected before, by the Master!

Wentworth pressed the flashlight into the man's hand.

133

The guard with the sword was driven violently... against the fat green belly of the god...

"When I cry *now!*" he whispered, "you will throw this light upon the Master!"

The man repeated the order fumblingly and Wentworth turned his head toward the altar and moved quietly from his side. Pain ran jaggedly through his breast when he saw Nita's plight. The two Chinese were binding her tightly across the stone pedestal. About him, the men laughed coarsely, Wentworth's lips closed bitterly. They would pay for this, every one of these dogs!

Nita....

Wentworth dared not allow his eyes or his thoughts linger upon her, lest even his steel self-control be snapped. Now that they had bound her to the altar, the Master would appear. And then....

Wentworth fastened his eyes on the altar, saw Nita's exquisite body helpless upon the stone. The two Chinese had stepped back. They looked unseeingly out over the white gangsters for a moment, then they turned and stalked behind the green god before which Nita was spread-eagled. The room was silent save for the lewd amusement of the sinister audience. Nita lay motionless, her eyes closed.

There was this lull of all action and thought and while it lasted, Wentworth stood like rock among the men. The gangster whom he had hypnotized stood rigidly, with the flashlight in his hand. Again Wentworth slipped his hand into his pocket where he had his Spider wig, and carefully folded silken cape. He would need them, and the fear they would create among these gangsters, who dreaded the swift vengeance of the Spider even more than death itself.

Wentworth was aware of rustlings among the silken curtains, and coldness crept along his spine. The sound reminded him of snakes crawling amid dead leaves. He knew then, past any doubting, that the Master was aware of Wentworth's presence in his stronghold and he was gathering his forces of evil behind the silken drapes. Not through Nita's betrayal, not through anything he himself had done… but because Nita's mere presence in this place meant that Wentworth could not be far away!

And they were tormenting her, to make him reveal himself!

He moved his shoulders an inch to make sure his holsters were free beneath his vest. He cast a secret glance beneath his lids toward the men about him. If they heard the rustlings behind the silk, they paid it no heed. All their attention was focused on Nita!

As Wentworth stared, the rustling stopped—and simultaneously, a half dozen of the Mongols, naked to the waist, filed out from behind the green god. After they had taken their places flanking the altar, another man walked out slowly, a giant with a naked heavy sword in his hands. The executioner!

He took his place by the altar beside Nita. His eyes gloated over her, and he reached down to touch a thumb gently to the edge of his blade. Afterward, he spat red betel juice upon his finger and drew a tantalizing red line across Nita's white throat!

Still the Master did not reveal himself!

THE MEN were quiet now, and Wentworth felt his muscles tighten with the urge to action—and he waited. He waited while

Nita rolled her head away from the threat of that glittering steel blade. Her eyes swept the waiting men. They did not hesitate when they touched Wentworth, but he read her gaze.

There was despair in them, but there was courage, too. Her eyes told him plainly: *My life is yours!*

Wentworth laid the bonds of his will upon himself through that next long minute while silence held. Then his breath gushed out in a long sigh. It seemed incredibly loud, until he realized that every other man in the room had sighed with him!

For suddenly, the Master was before them! He stood with folded arms at the head of the altar. A robe of crimson silk hung from his shoulders to the floor. His bald head was an evil thing, and there was a sneer on his thin mouth. But his eyes... Wentworth felt them sweep over him, and an oath struck against his locked teeth! The man was not the Master! He could not be mistaken by those eyes, though he had seen them only once!

Not the Master... but when he turned toward Nita, the executioner stepped back and lifted the sword!

Wentworth caught back the sob of desperation that leaped to his lips. This was not the Master, yet the Master must be in this very room! He would not trust an underling to contrive the capture of the Spider.

There was no alternative for Wentworth now. He must force the attack upon himself, hope in the mêlée to spot and slay the Master! Another moment's delay would accomplish nothing, save Nita's death!

The man in the crimson robe set his fist in Nita's hair, and yanked her head back. The long nails of his other hand bit into the flesh of her shoulder, and his eyes turned gloating to the executioner.

"*Shah!*" he hissed. "Kill!"

Wentworth sent his own whisper across the room. *"Now!"* he said sharply!

The man who held the flashlight lifted his hand like an automaton and brilliantly focused beam of the torch flashed out. Across the man in crimson and the executioner with the lifted sword, there fell a black shadow—a thing of hairy poised legs, and poison fangs—*the seal of the Spider!*

And while men stood, frozen motionless in the shock of fear that the shadow brought, the Spider laughed! He sent the sound of his laughter, flat and mocking, across the altar room.

"*The Spider takes vengeance!*" he whispered.

That moment, the paralysis of the men broke. They shouted and wheeled about. Behind Wentworth, the silken curtains shrieked thinly as the Mongol guards leaped forward. Glittering hatchets and honed knives were in their fists. But Wentworth's trickery had worked. The man with the flashlight in his hand stood like a man of stone, and it was upon him that the shouting killers hurled themselves!

Guns crashed. A hatchet whined through the air. In an instant, a dozen knives and hatchets, a score of bullets crashed into the man who threw the Spider's shadow upon the altar.

It gave Wentworth the moment he needed. While death whined and shrieked across the room, he whipped the wig down upon his head, hurled the long black cape across his shoulders! Its skirt kited out behind him, made him an enormous, menacing figure in the half-light of the room. His two guns were ready in his fists.

The Spider charged the altar!

The guns spat simultaneously, their thunder swallowed up in the fury of battle. But his bullets sped true. The giant with the sword was driven backward violently against the fat green belly of the god. The man who mimed the Master was hurled kicking to the floor, and his face was suddenly as crimson as his robe.

Two bounds took Wentworth to the altar. His flailing gun barrels drove one of the Mongol guards stunned with the violence of his attack headlong from his path. He snatched a knife from the belt of a corpse and with a swift sweep severed the ropes that bound Nita to the altar!

He heard a high, nasal voice call out furiously from somewhere amid that mêlée of slaughter.

"Fools!" it cried. "You have killed the wrong man! *The Spider is on the altar!*"

DEATH HOVERED in that screaming voice. Wentworth's eyes and ears quested for the man who spoke, even while he flung an arm around Nita. He thought the cry came from one of the half-naked Mongols. His bullet smashed the man's spine. Then he hurled himself and Nita flat to the floor behind the altar.

An instant later, a storm of lead swept above the cruel stone. Chips flew from the green idol—and the voice of the Master was still shrieking orders.

"Another gun in my pocket," Wentworth whispered to Nita. The guns in his hands were speaking even as he threw the words at her. They hammered out in a powerful, steady rhythm, and at each crash, the dimness of the room increased. His lead was smashing out each light in turn!

He could hear Nita's sobbing breath beside him, heard her gun speak, and the scream of the man her lead sought out. A hatchet skimmed across the top of the altar, clanged brazenly against the idol. Wentworth shot out the last light!

He caught Nita's arm and ducked with her behind the idol and waited in the maelstrom of terror and death.

"There should be a door here," Wentworth whispered. "Find it, while I stand guard!"

Nita left his side in an instant and Wentworth's guns snouted about the idol. He began to shoot at voices, at the flash of guns. He fired by the feel and balance of his guns, but it was the style of shooting he always employed. Darkness could offer no hindrance to him.

"Cease firing, fools!" the Master cried. "Move back against the wall. Move back, I tell you! There are enough of us to cover every exit! Move fast!"

Nita's hand touched Wentworth's arm in the dark. "There is no door here, Dick," she whispered.

Wentworth swore softly. "There was a trick used in the throne room," he said softly. "Climb up behind the idol and press both its eyes at the same time!"

Soon Nita's feet thudded to the floor beside him. "They moved!" she whispered.

Wentworth seized her hand and dodged backward against

the wall. This time his outflung hand found an opening and he turned sharply.

His brain raced on with the strategy that must be used. "You will run ahead and escape," he said swiftly. "There is a door in the concrete. There should be a lever on this side, though the outside mechanism is hidden. Summon the police. I will hold them here until you return. It is the only way, Nita! We cannot risk the escape of the Master!"

Nita gasped. "There is a phone in the shop, if I can reach it. Are we going that way?"

Suddenly, they found themselves in the antechamber of the altar room. There were no guards in sight.

"The door is in the center of the opposite wall," he said quietly. "The corridor is beyond." He flung a quick look about him. Against the far wall were two chests. They were the only possible barricade.

Wentworth whirled the two chests out from the wall, jammed them together for a barricade. He could hear the slap of running feet along the corridor they had traversed. The shouts of men echoed.

"Dick!" Nita cried. "I've found the lever, but it doesn't work!"

Wentworth leaped toward the sound of her voice, seized the lever and wrenched it. It gave without resistance! His eyes canvassed the wall. No doubt that this was the operating lever. A curse burned his lips.

"No use," he said harshly. "They've locked that door from the altar room. We're trapped! But so are they! Down, down, Nita behind those chests! Get your gun ready!"

WENTWORTH'S EYES roved frantically over the room, traced the lines of steam pipes that coursed the ceiling and vanished above. The thump of machinery still went on up over their heads.

"The lights!" he cried. "They must go up into the factory, too. There's a wire that runs along the base of the wall, Nita! Cut it with a bullet, and signal in Morse code by touching the ends together!"

Nita's smaller gun coughed and the lights blacked out in the room. An instant later, hot white sparks threw blue-white flares across the room.

Overhead the lights blinked and blinked, Wentworth dragged the chests back closer to the wall so that Nita was more fully sheltered. He waited… and heard the rasp of concrete across the room. The second door of the altar room was opening. Men rushed out in a pounding charge, half-naked Mongols with their threatening hatchets, and glistening knives; gangsters with heavy guns. A machine-gun stammered and cement dust powdered upward from the floor.

Wentworth crouched and fired coldly! Again and again Nita's smaller gun coughed at his side, and for that moment the lights remained burning brightly. Six shots cracked from behind the chests, and six men went down. The charge broke.

Nita's whisper reached him, softly. "I have only two more bullets, Dick. Have you any extras?"

Wentworth shook his head wordlessly. "Not for that gun," he said quietly. "I've started on my second clip. There's one more clip for each of them. Twelve more shots!"

Abruptly, the ceiling lights ceased to blink, and darkness settled thickly across the room. "The current's off," Nita whispered, and Wentworth felt her presence beside him. "I sent the message three times. Told them about the laundry shop. Told them to call the State Police… And, Dick, I told them the Spider was trapped here. Nothing else would bring them as quickly!"

Wentworth smiled in the darkness. "You are right, Nita," he whispered. "We have a moment left while they reform their lines."

"They took me so easily, Dick," she said softly. "Just walked up to the car and took me out. They must have suspected you."

Wentworth nodded. There was no doubt of that. Somewhere, he had slipped up in the ritual of identification….

Wentworth silenced Nita with a pressure on her shoulder. His ears must keep watch for him now. He caught the whisper of a naked foot in the darkness, and his gun lashed out its fury. The lurid powder-flash showed him three Mongols creeping toward him. He needed no more than that glimpse. His guns hammered out three swift shots. There were screams, and a hoarse moaning, then silence. And blackness. And waiting.

Three times, they tried to sneak upon Wentworth and Nita in the darkness, and three times the unerring lead of the Spider's guns drove them back and laid their dead upon the floor. Nita emptied her last bullets into the body of a huge Mongol whose hatchet almost reached them.

In the darkness, Wentworth fingered his last bullets. There were six. Two more charges would finish them.

SUDDENLY, THE Master's voice called tauntingly to them through the dark.

"Surrender, Spider!" it called. "And I promise you both a quick and easy death! Continue to fight, and you shall die as slowly as all my skill can contrive. And I warn you that I am skillful!"

Wentworth's guns quested with what seemed senses of their own for the direction of that voice, but he held his fire.

From the darkness, the Master laughed sneeringly. "So your ammunition runs low! It is as I thought. And I have many men, many guns. Surrender, Wentworth! Your signals to the police are in vain! I control the plant above us!"

Wentworth felt Nita close against him, heard her voice soft in his ear. "Dick. Oh, Dick… *save a bullet for me!*"

Wentworth caught another sound, and suddenly the darkness split again with his gunfire. Three times he hurled his bullets across the room, and three more men went down. But now there were only three bullets!

He did not think that the Master spoke the full truth. Undoubtedly, he controlled the plant above to some extent; but if he had full authority, there would be no need of this secret and heavily protected entrance from the Chinese laundry. Moreover, the flickering of the factory lights would have been visible from the town as well as within the plant itself. There was still hope that the police would come. But there was small hope they would find the Spider and his mate alive!

Wentworth narrowed his eyes and peered into the darkness beyond the lights. Dimly, he could make out a mass of men bunched for the charge! From behind them the Master's voice lifted once more, tauntingly.

"Your last chance, Wentworth!" he called. "I have guns here that will smash through your barricade. But we will not kill either of you... right away! You will be saved to die slowly. This is your last chance. *Will you surrender now!*"

Desperately, Wentworth sought an answer. If only he could make sure of the Master's death, he would risk an accounting with these others. He knew just where the Master was. His voice placed him definitely, but there was a barricade of living flesh in front of him. With only three bullets....

His eyes ranged frantically about the room. The Master cried out impatiently... and suddenly Wentworth pointed his gun toward the far corner of the ceiling, and squeezed the trigger. A steam pipe rang under the assault of the lead. Powder bounded from the concrete on the far wall. The Master laughed mockingly.

Once more, Wentworth fired, and once there was the clang of steel, the dusting of powder from the wall. Only one bullet now!

Nita pressed close beside him. She had asked for one bullet, for herself. The torture... But there was still hope.

Wentworth muttered to Nita. "Those are high-pressure steam pipes, used in the factory up there. Pressures of twelve hundred pounds are not unusual. If I can puncture one!"

"You have weakened that coupling you hit twice, Dick," she said slowly. "Try once more!"

Wentworth turned his head and looked into her eyes.

Across the room, the Master lifted his voice: *"This is your last chance!"*

"MY LAST bullet," Wentworth said quietly.

Nita gave him her smile, as her hand rested on his arm. "Shoot, Dick!" she said.

Wentworth faced forward.

There was once more the clang of steel, and dust leaped from the wall. For the moment, that was all. Wentworth dropped his guns.

"They promised us an easy death," he said slowly. "I do not know!"

Nita's voice caught in her throat. "There are knives there, Dick!"

Wentworth gathered his feet beneath him. His heart exulted in Nita's courage. Her hand rested on his arm and there was a smile on her mouth that matched the smile of the Spider.

"We are still together, Dick!" she whispered.

They set themselves to leap to the final attack… and there was a crack like the snap of tempered steel. The coupling clanged loose from the steam pipe, and there was a vibrant hiss that rose to a shriek. Nothing showed beside the high-pressure steam pipe… but the men on the floor beneath it screamed in sudden intolerable pain.

For an instant, one man stood exposed. One man, wrapped in a crimson robe that covered him from head to feet. His face was horribly contorted. His arms were thrust out wildly, and there was a scream in his throat.

While Wentworth and Nita watched, flame burst out about him. His flesh turned bright crimson, turned brown, then black.

The *Master* pitched forward to the floor and did not stir.

Suddenly, Wentworth became aware of a heavy pounding on the wall behind him. He heard sledges and the hammer of a pneumatic drill!

Wentworth turned to Nita and clasped her close. She clung to him, as shudders swept over her body. And in the room of death, Wentworth laughed, and presently went to press the seal of the Spider upon those dead who lay beyond reach of that awful jet of steam. Nita van Sloan rose to creep into his arms.

"It's the police," she said. "The police! And there is no way out!"

Wentworth shook his head at her. "Yes," he said, calmly. "The police have come… *for the Spider!* But the Master, the War Emperor is dead. It is worth it. Our country is safe now." He bent to kiss her lips. "The Spider is content!"

COMMISSIONER OF POLICE Kirkpatrick was late in returning to headquarters from the theatre opening he had attended. His secretary opened the door of his private office for him, grinned derisively.

"There's a message on your desk Commissioner," he said. "Some state cops up in New France think they've got the Spider trapped. They want you should come up and identify him."

Kirkpatrick snatched up the message. "Man, this is two hours old! Why didn't you get word to me at once!"

The secretary's face was ludicrous with surprise. "Geez, commissioner, I'm sorry," he stammered. "I didn't figure it was important enough to bother you! Look, I've got more dope on it here. Came in later. Some blinking lights called in the cops, said the Spider was trapped under some chink laundry. They broke in and found a flock of dead men, roasted to death with steam and shot up with bullets. There were a flock of Spider seals all around, and one guy had on the Spider cape. But, shucks, commissioner, you know the Spider doesn't get caught like that!"

Kirkpatrick's face was drawn. "There's always a last time, Cassidy," he said slowly. "Order my car at once. A motorcycle escort."

Cassidy ducked out the door, jarred it shut behind him. Kirkpatrick stood in the middle of the floor and looked down at the message. When he spoke, it was between stiff lips, as if the words forced themselves out against his will.

"God grant that it… isn't Wentworth!"

The door opened casually. "Asking for me, Kirk?" said the man in the doorway.

Kirkpatrick wheeled around, his face stiff with amazement. Then he laughed. There was thankfulness in his eyes.

"Dick!" he cried. "Thank God, Dick!"

Wentworth stood on the threshold with his brows lifted in curiosity. Nita laughed at his side. "Dick," she said, "Stanley actually seems glad to see you!"

Kirkpatrick strode forward, shook the message at Wentworth.

Wentworth said, "I understood you wanted me for questioning in a murder, Kirk. It's the first time I've had a chance to surrender!"

Kirkpatrick brushed the words away with a wave of his hand.

"An anonymous accusation," he said brusquely. "The man never came forward. But this... I guess there's no use in going up there. Cassidy was right. They'd never catch the Spider in a trap like that! Obviously, the Spider was there. Obviously, he has killed this spy who was tormenting us! Obviously... he was not there when the police arrived!"

Wentworth said, "May I see?" He skimmed through the message, shrugged and laughed. "Well, the Spider may have been there when the police arrived. After all, you weren't there to handle them, Kirk. He could easily have knocked out a cop, put on his uniform and... say to make an excuse for going back out of the place... carried along a body as if it were an injured... man. Then an ambulance. An old trick, Kirk."

Kirkpatrick's eyes rested on him keenly. "As you say, an old trick, Dick. You never leave any evidence, Dick. But someday you'll slip. When you do, I'll send you to the death house as surely as my name is Kirkpatrick!"

Wentworth lifted his brows, turned smiling to Nita. "Kirk is a hard man to convince, isn't he, my dear?"

Kirkpatrick flung an arm around the shoulders of each of them. Nita went white to the lips, but she still smiled.

"I think I'm happy," Kirkpatrick said, and his crisp tones were exuberant. "I was afraid... Dick, I didn't finish what I was saying. I'll send you to the death house. And afterward, I'll resign my office and... well, perhaps I'll join you!" He laughed, but his laughter did not hide the genuine truth behind his words. He would not swerve in his duty, but it would be death for him as well. Kirkpatrick shook them by the shoulders. "Come home with me. I have one more bottle of that 1809 Napoleon brandy. I think this is the night for it!"

Cassidy came bumbling back through the door. "Car's all ready, Commissioner. Motor cops on the way!"

Kirkpatrick stared at the man, without taking cognizance of his words for a moment. Then he nodded crisply. "Won't need them thanks, Cassidy," he said. "Dismiss… Oh, by the way, was there a report from New France of an ambulance stolen?"

Cassidy nodded alertly, "Yes, sir! Does that mean anything?"

Kirkpatrick shook his head. There was a smile about his grim mouth.

"Yes, Cassidy," he said quietly, "It means quite a lot. You may notify the State Police that they haven't got the Spider… this time!"

Wentworth offered his cigarette case, thumbed flame to his lighter. He was smiling, but his eyes were innocent.

"Elusive chap, this Spider, what?" he asked smoothly.

POPULAR HERO PULPS AVAILABLE NOW:

OPERATOR 5
❏ #1: The Masked Invasion $13.95
❏ #2: The Invisible Empire $13.95
❏ #3: The Yellow Scourge $13.95
❏ #4: The Melting Death $13.95
❏ #5: Cavern of the Damned $13.95
❏ #6: Master of Broken Men $13.95
❏ #7: Invasion of the Dark Legions $13.95
❏ #8: The Green Death Mists $13.95
❏ #9: Legions of Starvation $13.95
❏ #10: The Red Invader $13.95
❏ #11: The League of War-Monsters $13.95
❏ #12: The Army of the Dead $13.95
❏ #13: March of the Flame Marauders $13.95
❏ #14: Blood Reign of the Dictator $13.95
❏ #15: Invasion of the Yellow Warlords $13.95
❏ #16: Legions of the Death Master $13.95
❏ #17: Hosts of the Flaming Death $13.95
❏ #18: Invasion of the Crimson Death Cult $13.95
❏ #19: Attack of the Blizzard Men $13.95
❏ #20: Scourge of the Invisible Death $13.95
❏ #21: Raiders of the Red Death $13.95
❏ #22: War-Dogs of the Green Destroyer $13.95
❏ #23: Rockets From Hell $13.95
❏ #24: War-Masters from the Orient $13.95
❏ #25: Crime's Reign of Terror $13.95
❏ #26: Death's Ragged Army $13.95
❏ #27: Patriots' Death Battalion $13.95
❏ #28: The Bloody Forty-five Days $13.95
❏ #29: America's Plague Battalions $13.95
❏ #30: Liberty's Suicide Legions $13.95
❏ #31: Siege of the Thousand Patriots $13.95
❏ #32: Patriots' Death March $14.95
❏ #33: Revolt of the Lost Legions $14.95
❏ #34: Drums of Destruction $14.95
❏ #35: The Army Without a Country $14.95
❏ #36: The Bloody Frontiers $14.95
❏ #37: The Coming of the Mongol Hordes $14.95
❏ #38: The Siege That Brought Black Death $16.95
❏ #39: Revolt of the Devil Men $16.95
❏ #40: The Suicide Battalion $16.95
❏ #41: The Day of the Damned $16.95
❏ #42: The Dawn That Shook the World $16.95
❏ #43: When Hell Came to America $16.95
❏ *NEW:* #44: Invasion From the Sky $16.95

G-8 AND HIS BATTLE ACES
❏ #1: The Bat Staffel $13.95

CAPTAIN COMBAT
❏ #1: The Sky Beast of Berlin $13.95
❏ #2: Red Wings For the Blood Battalion $13.95
❏ #3: Low Ceiling For Nazi Hell Hawks $13.95

ACE G-MAN
❏ #1: The Suicide Squad Reports for Death $14.95
❏ #2: Coffins for the Suicide Squad $14.95
❏ #3: Shells for the Suicide Squad $14.95
❏ #4: The Suicide Squad in Corpse-Town $14.95
❏ #5: Wanted–In Three Pine Coffins $14.95
❏ #6: The Suicide Squad's Dawn Patrol $14.95
❏ #7: Targets for the Flaming Arrow $16.95

DUSTY AYRES AND HIS BATTLE BIRDS
❏ #1: Black Lightning! $13.95
❏ #2: Crimson Doom $13.95
❏ #3: The Purple Tornado $13.95
❏ #4: The Screaming Eye $13.95
❏ #5: The Green Thunderbolt $13.95
❏ #6: The Red Destroyer $13.95
❏ #7: The White Death $13.95
❏ #8: The Black Avenger $13.95
❏ #9: The Silver Typhoon $13.95
❏ #10: The Troposphere F-S $13.95
❏ #11: The Blue Cyclone $13.95
❏ #12: The Tesla Raiders $13.95

MAVERICKS
❏ #1: Five Against the Law $12.95
❏ #2: Mesquite Manhunters $12.95
❏ #3: Bait for the Lobo Pack $12.95
❏ #4: Doc Grimson's Outlaw Posse $12.95
❏ #5: Charlie Parr's Gunsmoke Cure $12.95

THE MYSTERIOUS WU FANG
❏ #1: The Case of the Six Coffins $12.95
❏ #2: The Case of the Scarlet Feather $12.95
❏ #3: The Case of the Yellow Mask $12.95
❏ #4: The Case of the Suicide Tomb $12.95
❏ #5: The Case of the Green Death $12.95
❏ #6: The Case of the Black Lotus $12.95
❏ #7: The Case of the Hidden Scourge $12.95

THE SECRET 6
❏ #1: The Red Shadow $13.95
❏ #2: House of Walking Corpses $13.95
❏ #3: The Monster Murders $13.95
❏ #4: The Golden Alligator $13.95

CAPTAIN ZERO
❏ #1: City of Deadly Sleep $13.95
❏ #2: The Mark of Zero! $13.95
❏ #3: The Golden Murder Syndicate $13.95

RED FINGER
❏ #1: Second-Hand Death $24.95